I0619156

CASSIE MINT

Big Boys: Books 5-8

BLACK CHERRY

PUBLISHING

Contents

III Big Beast

IV Big Brain

Keep in touch with Cassie!

Want to stay up to date with new releases, sales, and more instalove goodness?
   Sign up for Cassie's newsletter!

I

Big Bet

Description

I'm a burlesque showgirl. I dance for crowds of thousands every night.

But it's only one man's attention I crave.

Every night after our show, I make my way to the big casino. I weave my way through all the luxury and sin, heading for one table in particular.

He's a blackjack dealer. A big, burly cutie in a bow tie… and my best friend.

I've wanted him for so long, but I'm too scared to risk it. What if we lose everything we have?

But you know what? This is the city of risk-takers.

Maybe it's time I bet it all on love.

Aubrey

It's busy tonight. Packed full, the casino ripe to bursting with visitors. There are the out-of-towners, the folks who are here for the glitz and novelty—laying down small bets with big grins, sure as hell that they'll lose it all anyways, then laughing loudly at the thrill.

I like the out-of-towners. They don't kick up a fuss when they flush it all away.

Then there are the serious gamblers. The career folk. They put down measured bets, and the good ones win back more than they lose, and the bad ones slump over the bar and cry to the bartender. But, you know, even the good ones don't seem like they're having fun.

I guess they're not. I guess this is a job to them, same as anything else. I sure don't feel like dancing burlesque for one hundred percent of the time I'm on stage.

My least favorite groups are the stag parties. The groups of young men moving together like packs of hyenas, barely watching the tables because their gleaming eyes are probing the crowds.

Stag parties *always* have something to say to the burlesque girls. It's never anything we'd care to hear.

Rich or broke, relaxed or intense, it seems like every soul on the strip came here tonight. I swallow down my disappointment, weaving between plush green tables, nodding at the dealers in their crisp white shirts and bow ties when I recognize their faces.

It's not that I want the casino to do poorly. Or that I want Will to get fewer tips. It's just that I like the quieter nights best, the nights when I can pull up at his table and we can chat together in low voices. The nights when I can drag him out to the sticky-hot street and monopolize his breaks, all for me.

He says he doesn't mind. That he'd rather spend his breaks with me than do anything else anyway.

Will is a cutie that way.

I squeeze past a somber poker game, an island of calm and concentration in the sea of chaos. Everyone here is dressed extra fancy—in tuxedos and tailored suits for the men; jewel-toned cocktail dresses for the women. Most of the women are draped over the men's shoulders like ornate scarves, but a few are actually playing.

I push down my surge of envy, and I regret it even more when one of the women glances over, raking me from head to toe with derisive eyes.

Yeah, okay, I look kind of funny after the shows. I changed into a simple pale blue dress, just fancy enough to meet the casino's dress code, but I still have my stage makeup and bouffant hair.

There's no need to be rude, though. For all she knows, this is how I like to look.

5

My hackles are still up when I find Will's table, and the fact that there are no stools free—well, it's the cherry on the cake. I huff, grumpy enough now to stomp my foot like a tyrant, but when I catch a proper glimpse of Will, all those bad feelings melt away.

He stands a head taller than most of the men in here. Dark haired, with scruff on his strong jaw. And the crisp white shirt that all the dealers wear—it stretches across his massive chest and big belly.

Black suspenders strain at his shoulders, looking like they'd snap if he so much as shrugged. His bow tie nestles under his beard. Will looks like a giant from a fairy tale—like someone cut down his beanstalk, and now he has to work as a blackjack dealer among the humans.

One look at my favorite dealer, and I'm all gooey inside.

He's perfect. Inside and out.

Will hasn't seen me yet, so I take a moment to prepare. I smooth the crinkled fabric of my dress over my hips; I trace my thumbs under my eyes, checking for smeared makeup. The lights are soft away from the spotlights shining on the tables, and I linger for a long moment, building up my courage.

The casino smells like mingling perfumes and expensive drinks, and the faint whiff of cigar smoke.

There's a burst of laughter nearby. The rat-tat-tat of a spinning roulette wheel.

Nothing else for it. I'm sure not here to play the games.

I step up to Will's shoulder, facing the table, and let his arm brush against mine. Sparks race over my bare skin at the contact—at the heat of his arm beneath the fabric of his shirt. Green eyes flick down to me, then crinkle at the corners as he stifles a smile.

6

That's the only greeting I'll get. Will is in the middle of a game.

I half-watch for a while, my eyes resting on the table but my mind drifting elsewhere. I've been nervous all night, on edge ever since I nearly turned my ankle on stage in the second dance, but with Will's heat washing over my side, I'm finally calm.

It was scary, but it didn't *really* happen, so I'd do better to let it go.

I sigh and shuffle closer, pressing our arms tighter together.

If anyone else did this, cozying up to a dealer, they'd probably get accused of cheating and thrown out. But the bouncers here know me by now, and they know I'm never here to play.

I do buy drinks, though. Just so they don't get tired of me taking up space.

"Want something from the bar?" I murmur when Will's game finally breaks. The patrons slide off their stools, a couple beaming, most scowling at their loss, and almost immediately, fresh people take their place. Will can't drink alcohol on shift, but there's a coffee machine behind the bar that we're both obsessed with. It's so good, I bet it could fool the pickiest barista.

"I'll get them." Will's deep voice makes me shiver. He's nodding and smiling at the new players, but he's talking to me. "Stay right here."

Ha. As if I'd wander off. I've found Will, and I plan on super-gluing myself to his side for the rest of the night.

The other burlesque girls find it baffling. They switch between teasing me for it, and begging me to spend my free hours another way. To come with them to the fancy nightclubs and dance with powerful men, or to go watch a movie with the quieter girls. *He's just a dealer*, one of the headliners scoffed once, and it took everything in me not to poke her in the eye.

Will's not *just* anything. He's my best friend, but more than that—he's the man that keeps me up at night, tossing and turning.

I gnaw on my lip as he strides away for our coffees, and already my chest's aching without him.

You see?

How the hell could I ever stay away?

* * *

I've never played blackjack. Nor roulette. Honestly, I've never played any of the games in this casino. When I was younger, I used to play Texas hold 'em with my grandma, but we played for paperclips. Sometimes chocolate buttons if we were feeling flush.

The thought of laying down actual money—actual hard earned *wages*—on these tables makes me sweat behind the knees. I guess the people here don't have landlords breathing down their necks every month.

If I had money to throw away, I wouldn't spend it here. I'd try the fanciest sushi in the city, or I'd get a real massage, the kind with white fluffy robes and scented candles.

Will catches my eye as he cuts back through the crowd, the revelers flowing around him like a rock in a stream.

Maybe I'd spend it on Will, actually. On one of those coffee machines to keep in his apartment, or on tailored clothes to fit his massive frame.

"You're frowning." He nudges the warm china mug into my hand, his own already half-empty. A quick glance around the waiting players, and then his eyes are back on me. "Everything okay?"

I hum, lifting the mug for a sip. *Wow,* that's good. "Just thinking about how I'd spend my riches."

Will's mouth quirks up at one corner. Lord, his lopsided smile makes my knees weak.

"Riches? You holding out on me, Aubrey?"

I beam at him. "Maybe I am."

He knows I'm not. Will knows damn near everything about me, right down to the ugly blisters on my toes. He rubs my sore feet in the casino locker room some nights. Spreads antiseptic cream over the raw, broken skin.

"Well." Will hands his empty mug to a passing server, then turns back to the table. Starts to deal a new game. "Remember me when you're top of the pile, Aubrey James."

As if I could ever forget him.

This man is all I want in the whole wide world.

Will

By the end of my shift, Aubrey's wilting. She's got a stool at my table, finally, but her eyes are glazed over and her face is pale with exhaustion. I spent the last hour grinding my teeth, desperate to drag her out of here into the fresh air so I can coax her to eat something hot and then walk her home.

I don't know why she insists on coming here after her show. She must be dead on her feet after hours and hours of dancing. But she comes every night, all to wait by my side while I'm working—I can't even talk to her properly, damn it, but she comes anyway.

A selfish part of me is glad she does.

I miss her badly on the rare nights when life keeps her away.

I'm not an idiot. I know better than to let myself read into things—girls like Aubrey don't end up with big men like me. She's soft and pretty and kind, so gorgeous that she's hard to look at sometimes. Dazzling, like the diamonds draped around the rich ladies' necks.

10

She thinks of me as her friend. Nothing more. And though it burns me up inside, I'll take that much from her and be grateful for it. I'll take every scrap of Aubrey that I can.

The sky is tinged pink when we finally step onto the sidewalk. The whole strip's lit up bright, a huge array of pulsing lights, and palm tree fronds wave in the breeze. Even at dawn, the sidewalk's crowded and cars snake slowly through the streets, bumper to rattling bumper.

I take a deep breath. Here goes nothing.

"You could come back to my new place, if you like. It's a lot closer than yours." There's nothing funny about my offer, and god, I hope Aubrey knows that. I'd rather jump off a bridge than ever make her uncomfortable.

"New place?" She looks adorably confused. Sleepy and dazed. Strands of her red hair dance on the breeze and stick to her dewy cheeks. "You moved?"

Ah, yeah. I didn't tell her that yet. I don't know why—I guess it felt awkward.

Because I picked my new place to be nearer to the theater where she dances. Because the apartment has two bedrooms, and one of them is painted lilac, which I know is her favorite color.

Aubrey doesn't have to move in with me, or anything. I won't get greedy. But maybe on nights like this, when she's tired and doesn't want to walk for over forty minutes back to her place, she might let me take her home. Might let me tuck her away where I know she's safe, and where the kitchen's stocked with all her favorites.

"Yeah. I moved." Her eyebrows pinch together, and fuck, she looks hurt. I wasn't trying to keep *secrets*. I just figured she'd take one look at my new place and know I got it for her, then figure out why, and every time I thought about telling her, my courage drained away. "Want to see?"

Because there's putting off telling her, and then there's making her walk forty minutes home when there's no need. I'm a coward, but I'm not an asshole.

Aubrey lifts one shoulder, still bemused. "Um, I guess so. Sure."

I should be glad she agreed, but every step along the sidewalk feels like walking to the gallows. Because what if she figures it out—how I feel about her? What if she's horrified?

What if she doesn't want to see me anymore?

My feet drum against the concrete, and my heart thumps in my ears, and Aubrey hurries beside me, her pretty face pinched in thought.

* * *

"It's not much." I push the front door open, then step aside and let her go first. It may not be much, but this building is way nicer than my last place. I saved up my biggest tips for months for the deposit.

It was an easy decision. Aubrey deserves somewhere safe and light; somewhere with a bathtub and pretty views over the city.

And the knot eases in my throat when I hear her gasp. When Aubrey wanders into the living room, eyes wide as saucers as she spots the balcony. The corner sofa is soft leather; there's a breakfast bar and floor-length drapes.

"Oh my *god*. Will! This place is beautiful."

Relief, cool and calming, floods my chest.

She likes it. Good.

"You can change anything you like," I blurt without thinking. "You can paint the walls. Pick out new furniture, or whatever. I bought it, so. It's—mine."

Ours, I nearly said. In my head and my heart, this place is ours. Mine and Aubrey's.

She turns to face me, her big, blue eyes wide.

"You *bought* it? Secretly?"

Shit. Yeah. That relief dissipates, and I'm on edge again. "I wasn't sure I'd get it."

"But—"

"Do you like it?" I press.

That frown is back. "Of course I do."

"Then you can stay here whenever you like. I cut you a key. Come here any time, okay? Think of it as—as a second home."

Aubrey stares at me, and for a horrible moment I think I've gone wrong. Said the wrong thing, or let it slip how badly I want her. She's looking at me like she's never really seen me before, and as I watch, two spots of color burn across her cheeks.

"Aubrey?"

She shakes her head. Jerks it quickly from side to side, like she's shaking off a trance.

"I... that's so sweet, Will." Her mouth quirks in a wry smile. "The sweetest thing anyone's ever done for me." *Busted.* I open my mouth to deny it, but Aubrey beats me there. "Cutting me a key, I mean."

"Right." I shift my weight, the floorboards creaking. "You're welcome."

I've spent all night with Aubrey within arm's reach. I've felt her warmth pressed against my arm; when I passed her mugs of coffee in the casino, her fingertips brushed against mine.

13

But none of that prepares me for when she strides across the living room, face determined, and wraps her arms around my waist.

God.

She's so small, pressed up against my belly. My palm splays across her back, holding her in place, and when I bend my head, her flyaway hairs tickle my nose.

The crown of her head smells like hairspray. What does Aubrey smell like when she's not all done up for a show? What's her day-off scent like? Fuck, I need to know.

"What's this for?" I sound hoarse. My throat's tight. Me and Aubrey, we're comfortable around each other, but we don't do *this*. We don't line our bodies up, all slotted together from head to toe so I can feel every inch of her. Every dip and swell. If I laid down on top of her, I'd barely feel more.

I turn my hips slightly, so she won't feel the effect she has on me. The line of my cock surging in my dealer's suit pants. The part of me that's desperate to get even closer—close as can be.

Aubrey shrugs, the fabric of her dress rustling from the movement. Her voice is quiet. "Do I need a reason to hug you?"

No. Hell no.

I don't answer and squeeze her tighter instead, molding her against the bulk of my body.

Aubrey sighs and pillows her cheek on my chest. Beneath my rib cage, my heart thumps an unsteady beat. She does that to me. Knocks me off kilter.

I'm nothing like the men on the billboards outside. I'm not lean with six pack abs, dressed in designer clothes and a fancy watch, or clean shaven with perfect straight teeth. But they're not the ones who get to hug Aubrey James, are they? So who's the real winner?

"Promise me you'll come here." I swallow, tongue heavy. "Don't ever walk all the way home when you're tired, okay? Come here instead. Come here any time."

That's why I bought this place.

And it's all worth it when she nods; when my girl sighs happily and burrows closer, the tip of her nose squishing against my chest.

Maybe I'm not the kind of man Aubrey would date.

But I'll provide for her just the same.

Aubrey

❧

Three weeks later, I slump in my seat in the crowded theater dressing room, prodding at a bunch of pink roses in a vase. The dressing room is long with high ceilings, and all along one wall are mirrors studded with light bulbs and assigned dressing spaces. Girls chatter in their seats or pace up and down, half dressed, one or two of them carrying bouquets of flowers just like mine.

Us burlesque girls get a lot of admirers. Or our bodies do, anyways.

My dressing table is cleaner than most, but it's still kind of a bombsite, scattered with cherry red lipstick tubes and mascara wands around the base of the glass vase. I sigh, rolling my aching neck, and pluck up a few balled up tissues from tonight's show before tossing them in the wastepaper basket by my feet.

Thank god Will doesn't see this side of me. The messiness. The part of me that doesn't really care if I line up all my makeup tubes just right. He'd probably ask for his apartment key back.

I'd never be so slovenly in *his* space, though. Whenever I stay over, which is most nights these days, I always take extra care to pick up after myself. I'm like one of those campers, leaving only footprints—except not even that, because I kick my shoes off by the front door.

"Another admirer, huh?" My neighboring dancer nudges me from her seat—a girl with black hair and a nose stud called Sapphire.

Even though we've been dancing together for almost a year, I don't know if that's her real name or a stage name. At this point, I'm too scared of offending her to ask.

"Nope." I flip the attached card over among the stems. "Same guy again."

Sapphire whistles when she sees the name, because it's one we all know. A famous actor, taking a break from the silver screen to blow off steam in the city.

Well, he won't be blowing off steam with *me,* no matter how many roses he sends. That part of me is all for Will—if he ever feels like freaking taking it, anyway.

"You should go out with him." Sapphire runs a fingertip along the embossed edge of the card, the envy plain on her beautiful face. "*I* would."

I shrug, uneasy. "I'm just not interested."

Sapphire snorts. "Seriously? If not this guy, then *who?*"

I know exactly who, but Will meets me here after shows sometimes. The last thing I need is to start tongues wagging and paint a target on his back.

His broad, strong, perfect back.

"I'm not sure," I say airily, waving a manicured hand, then start to gather up my things into my tote bag. Us dancers all did our nails together on our break between shows this afternoon, and now my fingers are tipped with glossy cream nails. "I guess I'd want him to be tall. And handsome and kind." I'm getting dangerously close to describing Will, so I veer off course to cover my tracks, staring down into the depths of my bag to cover the lie. "Maybe a lawyer or a doctor. Someone fancy and slick."

"Wow." The rumbling voice behind me makes my heart lurch and stomach drop. I jerk my head up, my horrified gaze meeting Will's unreadable one in the mirror. My sweet blackjack dealer stands behind my chair, his bow tie dangling undone around his neck. "That's quite a list."

Shoot. Shoot shoot shoot.

I didn't—didn't *mean* any of that. Not the stuff about a lawyer or a doctor, anyway. I just wanted to throw Sapphire off, but now Will's got this shuttered look on his face. Like a metal door's come slamming down, blocking me off from his thoughts. He looms behind my chair, all burly chest and big hands and short dark beard, and just the sight of him is enough to make my insides squeeze.

"Hey, Will." Sapphire's voice is flirty as she spins in her chair to greet him, her bare, toned legs crossing at the knee.

I know she doesn't mean any harm—it's not like he's my boyfriend, or anything. But I can't help the way my teeth snap together, molars grinding.

"Did you know Aubrey's got a movie star sending her flowers?"

What the hell?

I glare at Sapphire, stuffing the last bits and pieces in my bag. I'd stuff her in there too, if I could.

"No," Will says, so deep and calm. "But I'm not surprised. Aubrey's a beautiful girl."

Joy and misery war in my chest.

Joy because any time Will says things like that about me—which is often—I feel like I might float up to the ceiling. Like fireworks are popping off inside my brain.

And misery because he doesn't mean anything by it. He *never* means anything by it, damn it. Will doesn't even care that another man has sent me flowers.

"You going out with him?" Green eyes watch me closely in the mirror.

I shake my head, throat tight. "I don't think so."

"Tell her she should," Sapphire prods, still smiling up at Will. *My* Will.

"You should," he says immediately. "If that's what you want, Aubrey. Instead of a lawyer or a doctor."

Ugh.

I shove to my feet, feeling about a thousand years old, instead of my actual twenty-three. It's not just the aching muscles and the blisters on my toes, either, or the late hour, nor the fact that I haven't been sleeping well lately. It's been impossible while I've known Will is only one room away, his soft breaths audible through the wall, close enough that I could tip toe out into the hall and call his name. Could nudge his bedroom door open and steal a peek at him.

"I'm not interested," I grind out, and I can't keep the bitterness from my tone. Will blinks, but Sapphire rolls her eyes, good-natured as ever.

"Don't date him, then." She swipes the roses off my dressing table and settles them on hers instead, then calls after our retreating backs, "Leave some of the good ones for me, Aubrey!"

Ha. Sapphire has plenty of admirers. She's just teasing me,

19

trying to make me crack a smile, but I'm too grouchy now to play along. I scowl the whole way out of the building, then harrumph my way down the starry sidewalk after Will toward his new apartment. My sneakers hit the sidewalk hard, my shoulders rounded and my jaw set, and when Will glances down at me, I can tell he's trying hard not to laugh.

"Never thought a famous admirer could piss someone off so much."

I hitch my tote bag higher on my shoulder, staring right ahead. "Well, I guess so."

"Aubrey," Will says.

I sniff, chin high.

"Aubrey."

I hate that he affects me so much; that I melt so easily for him. Especially when he rumbles, "Don't be mad." And there's no humor when I glance up. Only a frown, creasing that broad, beautiful forehead.

His forehead. I'm waxing lyrical over the man's *forehead*.

Lord, I need an intervention. Therapy. Something.

"I don't want to date that guy."

"Okay," Will agrees, nonplussed. "Then don't."

But he doesn't say what I want to hear. He doesn't add, *date me instead*, and I'm starting to think he never will. That I'll grow old and die without feeling what it's like to be loved by this man. To know what his lips taste like.

"Do you like Sapphire?" I blurt. I can't stand not knowing. Because what if he dates her? What if he starts picking her up from the dressing room instead of me, and I have to watch them holding hands? Watch her sitting in his lap? Have to stay away from his apartment, because it's her territory now?

I'd leave the state. Maybe go on tour with a show, dragging

my broken heart around the biggest cities in America. Throw myself into dancing, and never set foot in a casino ever again.

"No." Will stares at me, throat bobbing as he swallows. The breeze tugs at his thick, dark hair, and limos rumble past in the road. Gosh, he's so handsome. Rugged and strong. *He* should be up on those billboards, not those delicate, pretty men that star in films. "Of course not."

Of course not. Well fine, if that's all he'll give me, I'll take it. I sigh and hook my arm in his, falling into step beside him.

"You should rent out your spare room," I murmur absently. It's been bothering me—knowing I could be costing him money. He could have another person in there if I weren't taking up so much space, imposing on his generosity. Hogging his spare key.

"But you use it."

"Yeah, but I don't *have* to."

Will tilts his head toward me as we walk, his voice dropping lower, and I stare at the moon as he speaks. "I like having you there, Aubrey. I'm not gonna rent it out."

Warmth seeps under my skin.

"Okay."

Will huffs a laugh. "Yeah. Okay."

It's not all settled, not really, but we've somehow found our way back to a good place for now. A place where I can push down all the longing, and chat to him like a normal human being. Like a friend.

It hurts, I muse, as we cross the lobby of Will's building. Being in love with someone who doesn't love you back. It's like waiting for a letter that will never come. Having a painful conversation by yourself.

He's worth it, though. When we pile into the elevator

21

together, I get a whiff of Will's scent: soap and beard oil and the fresh air from our walk home. There's a faint hint of the smoke from the casino clinging to him too, and even that makes my heart lurch. I don't even *like* the smell of cigars, but on him, it's like the world's best cologne.

I'll push down the pain to be around this man.

He's the only one for me.

* * *

I sit bolt upright in Will's spare bed, sweat cooling on my skin under my borrowed t-shirt. My heart's galloping a hundred miles an hour, and I suck down uneven breaths like I've been sprinting, not sleeping.

My hand trembles as I reach for the glass of water on my—on *Will's*—nightstand, and I gulp from it unsteadily.

Holy cow. I feel like I've been struck by lightning.

The blankets are puddled around my waist, and the glowing lights of the city seep around the edges of the curtains and cast funny shadows on the wall. I *love* this room—I feel more at home in this apartment than my own—but right now, I wish I could teleport back to my own bed. Away from these sheets that smell like Will's detergent; the soft sounds of his breathing in the next room; the thought that shocked me awake at… three AM.

I stare at the clock, dry-eyed. Gradually, with several deep breaths, my heart slows—but the dream doesn't leave me, bouncing around my tired brain.

I'd walked into the theater dressing room, though in my dream, the room stretched on forever, all the way to a distant horizon. The mirrors were all there like normal, but they were warped, like fun-house mirrors. They stretched me as I approached. Made me look like a whole other person.

And in my seat at my dressing table sat Will, facing the other way. Unmoving. Sapphire was perched on his lap, pressing a pink rose to her nose and inhaling deeply, kicking her crossed legs. When she caught sight of me over Will's shoulder, she almost looked sorry.

"It could have been you," the dream-Sapphire said, her voice lower than usual. All wrong. "But you never told him how you felt, did you?"

I woke up with his name on my lips.

Will.

I couldn't really tell him. Couldn't risk everything we have. Could I?

The room is humid as I swing my legs out of bed. I pad across the rug, peering through a crack in the curtains at the city before glancing back at my rumpled sheets, stomach sinking.

Nope. No way. I'm not getting back in there, not tonight. That bed freaking betrayed me. And at three AM nothing feels quite real, so I guess that's why I let my legs carry me out of the guest bedroom.

The living room is silent. Ghostly. And the steady sounds of Will's breaths get louder as I tiptoe to his bedroom.

The door swings open easily. Almost like he left it cracked open for me. As I cross the room, Will shifts in his sleep, turning onto his side to face the empty half of the bed.

I flip the sheets back quickly, forcing away the warning sirens clamoring in my head. The mattress dips beneath my weight, and then I'm laid out flat. Staring up at the ceiling.

"Aubrey," Will mumbles, and I'm not even sure he's awake. Then a hand reaches out, and I'm tugged toward him until I roll over, cuddling into his big chest.

A heavy palm smooths over my back, soothing my racing pulse, and I sigh. Melt closer until our bodies blur together.

"Bad dream?" His deep voice is thick with sleep. I nod, hair shifting on the pillow.

"The worst."

Will grunts, and I'm not one hundred percent sure, but I think maybe he kisses the top of my head. I like to think so, anyway.

"Stay here tonight."

Well, duh. I wriggle closer, his palm still rubbing my shoulder blades. "I'm on it, cap'n."

Will rumbles a laugh, and it's the first time I've *felt* it as well as heard it. It vibrates through my whole body, right down to my bones, and god, he'd have to peel me out of this bed with a crowbar. He'd have to force me out of here at knife point, and I tell him so.

"Hardly." Even scratchy and tired, Will's voice is dry. "I'd be more likely to tie you to the bed frame while you sleep, Aubrey. To never let you leave."

I wish.

The thought bounces around my head long after his breaths deepen again.

I wish. I wish. I wish.

Will

~~~~

There's something going on with Aubrey. For the last two weeks, she's been acting… funny, I guess. What else can I call it when she's crawling into bed with me every night? When she's hopping up onto the breakfast bar in her skimpy pajamas every morning, heels kicking against the cabinets as I make us brunch?

Aubrey's acting like—well, like she's my girlfriend.

And it's messing with my brain.

Tonight's no different. It's one of those rare nights when we're both off from work, when the stars align and our schedules match and we have long, uninterrupted hours stretching out in front of us. Normally, I love these days. I fucking *pray* for these days. A whole day off with Aubrey? Are you kidding me? I'd chop off a pinkie finger for one of those.

But normally, Aubrey's clear about our boundaries. She doesn't lean in for extra long hugs, or let her gaze rove over my body as if she likes what she sees. Normally, she's not testing my last scrap of control.

It's not real. I keep reminding myself that. Whatever this is—pity, or boredom, or even curiosity—it's not real. Aubrey doesn't want me the way I want her. If she did, surely I'd know by now.

It's not like I've kept my own devotion to her a secret.

"Thriller or Rom Com?" Her husky voice floats from my couch, where she's sitting cross-legged in a nest of blankets. Aubrey's flicking through movies on the TV screen, the remote gripped in her delicate hand. Wisps of steam curl from two mugs of brandy hot chocolate on the side table, and a bowl of popcorn is wedged beside Aubrey's knee.

I hover behind the couch. Trying to buy some time before I get into—into *that*. The nest of temptation. Devil nest.

"Thriller." The word grates out of me. The less *love* we watch on that screen, the better.

"It's so good not to be dancing tonight." Almost as soon as I've lowered to the couch, Aubrey wiggles around and stretches her legs out over my lap. Her feet are covered in fluffy socks, but I know what she's talking about. I've seen the carnage under there.

"Poor toes." Automatically, my thumbs dig into her arches. Knead away some of the tension.

And Aubrey purrs like a fucking cat.

"Mm." She settles back against the cushions in her skimpy white pajamas, eyes heavy and a satisfied curl to her lip. Her wavy red hair's twisted in a knot on her head, and her face is bare of makeup, the tiny beauty spot in the corner of her lip standing out more than usual.

So pretty. So perfect. So out of my league.

My heart thuds harder against my rib cage as she gives another little moan, and I swallow thickly as I keep rubbing her feet.

Not real.

Not real.

"Should we put the movie on?" Aubrey sounds kind of breathless.

"Right. Yeah." I fumble for the remote, clicking play before tossing it into the blankets and returning my hand to her foot.

Does it make me a bad guy to touch her like this? She clearly likes it—she's practically squirming all over the cushions, panting and flushing—but Aubrey doesn't know what *I'm* getting out of it. She doesn't know my pulse is racing, and my skin has flushed hot, and there's a steel rod in my pants which, if she shifted her feet, would give everything away.

Maybe if she knew that shit, she'd push me off, horrified. Maybe I'm taking advantage of her.

Fuck.

"Why'd you stop?" Aubrey murmurs when I cross my arms over my chest, hands balled into fists.

I stare at the screen, jaw tight. "Thumbs are cramping."

"Oh." She plucks at the blanket, then draws her legs off my lap and whispers, "Sorry."

She has nothing to be sorry about. Nothing in the whole damn world.

I glare at the screen and wait for explosions.

* * *

Partway through the second movie of the night, Aubrey swivels on the couch. She's been restless all evening, huffing and rearranging herself like a kitten that can't settle, and now she slides closer to me. Picks up my heavy arm and wriggles under it, draping my limb around her shoulder so my hand dangles down her body.

"Comfy?" I don't look at her. I can't. Not when the coconut scent of her shampoo washes over me, and every muscle in my body tenses, screaming to drag her closer.

"Mm." Her noncommittal hum is soft. Almost sad. Without thinking, I gather her against me. Rub my thumb back and forth against her hip.

A gentle sigh.

"That's nice." Aubrey buries her face in my chest, and fuck, she's not even pretending to watch the movie any more. She's just cuddling me, her hands fisted in my black t-shirt, and my blood pounds in my ears as I fight all my worst urges.

I want to *sniff* her.

To run my palms all over her body, feeling every inch.

I want to flip her over on this couch and lay down on top of her.

I want to break down every wall I've ever built between us, and show Aubrey she's more than my best friend. So much more.

"It's getting late." My voice sounds weird. *Off.* "We should get some sleep."

Aubrey sighs, but this time the sound isn't blissful. This time, it's like I can hear every ounce of her sadness and exhaustion.

"Aubrey?"

"What if we didn't?" she asks suddenly, voice hard. Shit, where did I go wrong? "What if we didn't get any sleep, Will?"

I blink, confused, but then she sits up and shrugs off my arm. Scrambles into my lap, knees sinking into the cushions on either sides of my hips, and *fuck*, Aubrey is straddling me. Gripping the sides of my face.

I've dreamed of this so many times. Pictured the weight of her, the soft give of her curves, the delicious way she smells—

I stare up at her like the world's biggest dumb ass. "What are you...?"

Aubrey scowls, her features set in a pretty frown, then dips her head. Presses a whisper of a kiss against my mouth.

It's so light. So quick. There and gone again, sending a shower of sparks crackling down my spine. If she didn't sit back and stare at me, waiting for my reaction, I'd think I dreamed it.

"Aubrey?" I manage. My heart's thumping and squeezing so hard, I'm kind of worried. Is this what a heart attack feels like?

"Nothing?" Her hands tighten in my shirt. "You felt nothing?"

She's still frowning, and I shake my head, still so fucking confused. My brain short circuited the second she climbed into my lap. What was the question?

"No, I—"

"Alright." Aubrey scrambles back off my thighs and stands in the center of the rug. She wraps her arms around her waist, and she looks so tiny, silhouetted in the glow of the movie. She heaves a sigh. "I, um. I'm sorry, Will."

"It's okay," I say quickly, but she's already turned on her heel. Her bare legs flash in the gloom as Aubrey marches to the guest room. "You don't need to—please don't go. Aubrey!"

The door closes with a gentle snap. I almost wish she'd slammed it. That's what I need right now—doors slammed in my faces and a bucket of ice over my head for good measure.

Aubrey—Aubrey kissed me. She kissed me and asked if I felt something.

29

Jesus Christ.
How did I mess this up?

Aubrey

I s there anything more tragic than a broken-hearted burlesque dancer? I sure don't feel like swinging my hips and peeling off my gloves tonight, I'll tell you that for free. I slipped out of Will's apartment before dawn this morning, but I've been keyed up all day. Tensed and on edge with the horror of what I've done.

I ruined the best friendship I've ever had.

He welcomed me into his home, cut me a key, and how did I repay him? I straddled him on his couch, practically mauled the poor man, and kissed him.

I should be ashamed of myself. I *am* so ashamed.

I left Will's key on the breakfast bar on my way out. There was no note; I didn't know what to say. How can I ever apologize enough for something like that? Words aren't big enough. Lord, I'm such a fool.

"You look like a kicked puppy, hon." Sapphire frowns at me, her sculpted eyebrows pinched with concern as we file into the dressing room after the show. I shrug, too tired to come up with some bullshit story, and not in the mood to talk to my dressing room neighbor.

It's unfair of me. That wasn't *really* her in my dream, and all this girl's ever done is tease me some and try to coax me out for cocktails.

But I guess I'm just a straight-up asshole now.

"It's nothing," I mutter, snatching the blue silk robe off the back of my chair and shoving my arms through the sleeves. I want this body of mine *covered*. God, I never want to look sexy ever again.

"Is it your man?"

I glare at the fresh vase of pink roses. Jeez, can't that guy take a hint?

"I told you." My chair rattles over the floor as I tug it out. "I'm not going to date him. I don't care if he's famous."

And I don't care if Will doesn't feel the same way. I love *him*, so that's that.

Gah.

"Not the actor." Sapphire watches me flop into my seat, grumpy and ungainly. I snatch up a tissue, dabbing at the thick makeup caking my face. "Your blackjack dealer."

I freeze, tissue pressed to my forehead. "...Will?"

Sapphire snorts. "How many blackjack dealers do you have a huge crush on, Aubrey?"

Rage punches me in the chest, stealing my breath. My cheeks burn hot, and gosh, if I weren't tensed into a statue, I might tackle this girl to the ground. "You *knew*? Then why the hell did you flirt with him?"

Sapphire shrugs, so unbothered, then sinks into her own chair and spins to face the mirror. "You two would've grown old and never told each other the truth. You'd be in the same freaking nursing home, sending longing glances across your TV dinners. I just nudged you along."

Huh. I guess she did. Slowly, my body comes back to life, and I start dabbing at my forehead again.

"It didn't work," I tell her quietly a few minutes later, when my anger's faded and I'm blotting out my cherry red lipstick. "I kissed Will last night. He turned me down."

Sapphire's outraged expression warms my poor, bruised heart.

"He did *what*? What the hell is that man thinking?"

"That he has free will?" I say dully. Why did I start this conversation up again? It does nothing but make me ache. I snatch my tote bag off the back of my chair and start stuffing bits and pieces inside. "It's fine. Okay? I'll get over it." *Lies.* "But first I'm gonna eat the biggest tub of ice cream I can find."

"That's my girl." Sapphire nods at me in the mirror, satisfied. "Put hot fudge sauce on it too."

"Good call."

Even though my tote bag's packed, I linger in the dressing room a while longer, watching Sapphire methodically wipe the makeup off her face.

I'll go out there in a second. Back into the world.

But I'll sit here for a while first. I'm so tired.

* * *

I've never been in the dressing room alone before. Not after hours, anyway, when the backstage corridors are silent and no music pulses from the stage. It's kind of spooky, if I'm honest. Half the mirrors are lit up, and half aren't, and the lights cast weird shadows across the floor. All the dressing

33

tables are still messy, abandoned with makeup tubes and hairbrushes scattered everywhere, like there was a bomb siren and everyone ran away mid-task.

I chew on my bottom lip, leaning back in my chair until it creaks. A borrowed magazine from three tables down is spread over my legs, and my feet are propped on Sapphire's chair.

It's not like I've got somewhere to rush to. And since I messed things up with Will, that forty minute walk home makes my feet throb just thinking about it.

Cookie dough ice cream, I decide. Or mint chocolate chip? My sigh makes the flyaway strands of my hair dance against my forehead, and I flick through the glossy magazine pages.

Whenever I get ice cream with Will, he picks whichever flavor was my second choice, then lets me share it. One time, we were messing around and I nudged his cone up and got ice cream in his beard, and he wasn't even mad. He laughed, his eyes crinkling at the corners, and dabbed it away with a napkin.

I had to bite my lip to keep myself from offering to lick him clean. Lord, I'd love to lick that man's whole big, beautiful body. I'd love to curl up and nap on his chest like a kitten. And—

No.

I can't think of him that way anymore. I need to respect Will's decision.

I flick past another few pages. It's all the same stuff—hair care, this season's trends, ways to blow your man's mind. I flick faster and faster, but it's all the same, and I could *scream*—

A floorboard creaks in the corridor.

I freeze, heart thumping.

I'm alone here. Holy crap, I'm all alone, and no one knows to look for me. What was I thinking, lingering in a dark, empty building like this? Tired feet are no excuse, and now I'm trapped in this dressing room with a strange person in that corridor.

I clear my throat. "Um. Hello?"

There's another creak, and when a large body steps into the doorway, I flatten my palm over my racing heartbeat.

"*Will.* You scared me!"

"Sorry." My best friend holds up his palms in surrender. "I didn't mean to lurk. But you didn't come to the stage door, so I came looking for you."

Silence spreads through the room. The last time I saw this man, he told me he felt nothing for me.

I swallow, throat dry. "You don't need to meet me at the stage door anymore. I can get home by myself."

"It's dark out—"

I choke out a laugh. "It's never *that* dark on the strip." It's true, too. The city lights are so bright, they pulse behind my eyelids when I close my eyes in bed.

"Aubrey," he says, and the pleading in his voice makes me *ache.*

I'd do anything for this man. But I can't pine after him like this anymore. It's not healthy.

"I'll catch a bus." My chair screeches over the floor as I stand and turn to face him square on. My tote bag bumps against my hip as I shoulder it. "Okay? I'll be careful, Will, I promise. But I need some… some space. I really do."

To lick my wounds. To nurse my broken heart. To get back to a place where we can be friends again—*real* friends this time.

"Aubrey." It's like he didn't even hear me. Will steps forward, his face determined, and god, he's so handsome in his dealer's shirt and bow tie. Those suspenders make his shoulders look wider than a building. "Last night—"

"I shouldn't have done it. I'm sorry."

"Yes," he interrupts, dragging a hand through his dark hair. It rucks up at the back, and I bite my lip, staring at the man I love as he steps forward, agitated. "You should have. Do you know how long I've wanted to do that, Aubrey? How long I've wanted to kiss you? And it happened so fast, I fucking missed it."

Will hardly ever curses around me. I blink at him, his words ringing in my head.

He wanted to kiss me?

He wanted me to do that?

My tote bag strap is digging into my collarbone. I adjust it, drawing in a slow breath.

"I—I *asked* you if you felt anything."

He nods, miserable. "I couldn't think straight. That's what you do to me, okay? You turn my brain to fucking mush. I had barely realized you were in my lap, that you were *touching* me like that, and then I'd said all the wrong things and you were already gone."

I guess I did kind of rush through it all last night. I was just so nervous. Every cell in my body was screaming, *fight or flight!*

It's funny. Burlesque is all about slow and steady seduction; drawing things out, making the audience drunk on anticipation. Teasing. Savoring. Going *slow.*

Then I was in and out of Will's lap last night faster than squirrel up a tree.

36

"Can we, uh." Will's deep voice jolts me back to the present. "Is there any chance we can try this again?"

I stare at the man I've wanted for so long. And he stares back, his chest heaving under his crisp white shirt.

Will stares at me with soul-deep longing splashed over his face. It's like seeing every ounce of my love for him mirrored back to me, except on thick, dark eyebrows and a strong nose and a clenched, masculine jaw.

Those green eyes bore all the way to my core. There's an answering tug between my legs, and then I'm restless, squeezing my thighs together against the tickly sensation, the trickle of heat.

Holy cow.

All he's done is look at me, and I'm already a puddle of goo.

"Here?" I squeak, because let's be honest, this is happening. I could no more resist this man than a hot fudge sundae on a summer's day. But if I could choose, I'd probably try this again somewhere that smells less like feet.

Will glances around the dressing room. His eyes land on the fresh bunch of roses from that actor, and a scowl settles over his features.

"Not here," he grits out, but his face gentles when he turns back to me. He stretches out a big hand, and finally, *finally,* I feel his thick fingers dwarf mine. "Come home, Aubrey. Please. I can't stand that place without you there."

I scoff as he tugs me to the doorway, but little happy fireworks are exploding inside me. "It's been less than a day, Will."

"I know. It's been hell."

Will

◦❧◦

"I bought this place for you." Aubrey splutters behind me as I turn the key in the lock, but I feel lighter. It's good to get this off my chest. "I was hoping you'd move in. To the lilac guest room, I mean. I never dreamed..."

Two small hands push gently against my back. "Inside, Will."

Right. Better not declare my love for all the neighbors to hear. I push the door open, holding it wide for Aubrey before following.

She sails inside like the lady of the manor. And she *is*. The lady of my apartment, anyway.

"Do you want to shower first?" I cringe as soon as the words leave my mouth, Aubrey's eyebrow ticking up her forehead. "Not that I'm expecting we'll do anything. It's just, I know that hairspray bothers you when you leave it in. But you don't have to, obviously. I don't care either way. Hell, I'd want you even if you were covered in grime—"

Aubrey takes mercy on me, thank fuck. She flicks my shoulder, mouth curling, then drifts toward the bathroom.

38

"Good idea," she calls over her shoulder. "I won't be long."

No. Good. Fine.

It's probably better if she takes a while. It'll give me a chance to slam my head against the wall a few dozen times. Apparently I need to reset my whole brain.

Honestly, for all my nervous rambling, I kind of wish *I* could take a shower. Not that—I *don't* expect anything, damn it, but I've just worked a full shift. The faint smell of cigar smoke and expensive gin always clings to my clothes after hours in the casino.

I can't help it. Aubrey makes me so nervous; she always has.

The stakes are so fucking high with her. Even on the first night we met, standing in line for extra strong coffees with the rest of the late night workers, I knew that she was it for me. The girl I wanted to be my wife.

"Will?"

My name floats through the apartment. Aubrey sounds shy at last, her voice thready and unsure.

I stride into the living room. "In here."

Better to keep this on neutral ground for now. If I drag Aubrey into my bedroom for this, she'll think I want something small with her. Something quick and meaningless.

Absolutely fucking not.

The sight of her inching into the living room steals my breath. Her hair's darker from the shower, swept over one shoulder as she squeezes the ends with a towel. Aubrey's skin is pink, scrubbed raw, and steam seeps after her like scented mist. She's dressed in one of my old t-shirts, a gray marl college shirt that hangs almost to her knees, and the fact that she had it in there ready means it was in her tote.

God.

I fucking love when Aubrey steals my clothes. She's always embarrassed when she's caught, but it makes me want to pound on my chest like a caveman.

"Sorry about…" She waves an awkward hand at the t-shirt. A big damp spot darkens the fabric, seeping wider where it touches her wet hair.

"I don't mind."

"You don't?" Aubrey brightens, skipping forward. "That's nice. You can borrow my stuff too."

I grin, suddenly giddy. "Maybe I will. Maybe I'll wear your pajama shorts like a hat."

Her snort feels like I've won the casino jackpot.

Then her smile fades away, and we're left standing in silence. The air's thick. Humming with promise. We've been building to this all night—no, since the day we met—but now that we're finally here, I don't know how to begin.

But Aubrey's looking at me, beseeching, twisting the hem of her stolen t-shirt, and I won't let her down again. Never again.

"Come here." It's gruff. Abrupt. But Aubrey trips toward me over the rug like I've read her a damn sonnet.

The living room's small, an open plan space that bleeds into the kitchen. A standing lamp casts a warm glow, and pearly white drapes hang in front of the glass balcony doors. Through the sheer fabric, the lights of the city burn yellow and blue, but it's just the two of us and the blank TV screen on the wall; the ghostly shapes of the sofa and a corner bookcase.

Aubrey's towel is warm and damp when I pull it gently out of her grip. It lands with a muffled thump on the rug, and her cheek is soft when I cup it with one hand.

"I want to kiss you, Aubrey." Her hair tickles my wrist.

40

"Properly this time." I thought when I finally said those words aloud, they'd sound awkward. Clunky. And maybe it's because I've said them so many times in my head, wearing the grooves of them over and over in my brain, but the words spill out easily. So natural.

Aubrey sucks in a sharp breath, then grips my wrist where I'm cradling her face. She clings to me, as if she needs the help to balance, and whispers, "Yes, please."

* * *

No rushing this time. I'm not a fool—I know that this is my best shot with Aubrey James. I won't fuck it up by slamming my mouth down on hers, rough and clumsy, no matter how badly my body wants to.

I trace the pad of my thumb over her cheek, drawing a line to the corner of her mouth. Swoop up to circle that beauty spot—that gorgeous mark that keeps me up at night. And then, heart drumming, I swipe my thumb along her plump bottom lip, pushing gently at the pillowy flesh.

Aubrey's lips part on an inhale. I nudge my thumb into the gap. Not all the way into her mouth—just resting at the entrance.

I wait, blood rushing.

She gazes up at me, eyes wide.

A hot, wet tongue lashes over the tip of my thumb. It's a tiny lick—a flutter of contact—but it's enough to tear a groan from my chest, and when she nips me next, her pearly teeth surprisingly sharp... forget it.

"Aubrey."

I watch, breathless, as she sucks my thumb into her mouth.

She suckles me lazily, her eyes lidded, and her pupils are blown wide.

Fuck, she wants this as much as I do.

"Aubrey," I grate out.

Her hum tingles against my thumb. "Mhm?"

"I want to..." I stop, trying to catch my breath. Trying to remember the lecture I gave myself as we walked here. The one about restraint, and not rushing her, and taking nothing for granted. "I want to do this right."

Her lips curl around my thumb in a wicked smile. "You don't like this?" The disbelief is clear in her tone, and fuck, she's right. My cock is harder than granite.

"I like it." It takes every ounce of self control, but I ease my thumb from between her lips. She lets me go with a wet pop that makes my hands twitch. "I fucking love it. But I want to do this properly, okay? I want to kiss you, like I said. This is not just a hookup. Not to me."

Irritation flashes over her pretty features, but then Aubrey huffs and cups my cheek. My beard bristles audibly against her palm. "It's not a hookup to me, either. Will. This is it."

Yeah. This is it, alright. So I draw in a deep breath, then lower my head.

Soft.

She's softer than I'd dreamed. Soft and sweet and warm and delicious, melting into me with a sigh. Aubrey parts her lips easily, welcoming me inside, and as our tongues stroke together, she flattens her little body against my front.

Against my barrel chest.

My rounded belly.

Self-consciousness rises up inside me like a tide, but then Aubrey rocks up onto her toes; sinks her hands into my hair and nips at my bottom lip.

"Finally," she groans, and how can I doubt that she wants me? It's clear the hungry way she kisses me, so greedy, like when she raids the freezer for ice cream after a long day. It's in the pulse I can feel racing under the soft skin of her throat.

If Aubrey wants me like this, that's all that matters. She could have a guy with six pack abs if she wanted. Even that famous actor.

But she chose a guy who can throw his weight around.

"Will!" My name squeaks out of her as I snatch her up, balancing her ass in my hands. I can't help kneading her, groaning into her mouth, and Aubrey hooks her ankles behind my back.

"So fucking perfect, baby."

I picked her up instinctively, but where the hell am I planning on taking her? There are only the bedrooms or the bathroom, and none of those rooms would help with my plan not to rush things. So I spin in place, then lower us onto the sofa, the frame creaking under our joined weight.

"*Will.*" Slender hands scrabble at my belt buckle. The thought of her cream-painted nails wrapped around my cock makes my teeth grind.

"Wait." I flatten a palm over my waist, trapping her hands. "Aubrey, slow down."

She stiffens, and I lean back just in time to see hurt flash over her face. "Um. You don't want to?"

Aubrey

❧❧❧

"**D**on't want to?" Will's mouth tugs up at the corner. He stares at me in disbelief. "Don't I *want* to? Aubrey. This is all I've fucking wanted since the day I met you."

Oh. Good. Likewise.

"So why can't we—"

"Because I know…" Will trails off, his cheeks flushing pink above his beard. And for the first time since we got here, he won't meet my eye. He stares over my shoulder instead, one palm still flattening my hand against his belt. "I know you haven't done this before. And I don't want you to feel rushed."

Huh. Yeah, that's the problem with me and Will. He's my best friend, and I tell him *everything*. Never thought it'd bite me in the ass like this, though.

"Years of wanting each other is hardly rushing, Will."

His shoulders are so broad that when he shrugs, it's like the landscape shifting. Like the earthquakes we get sometimes back where I grew up.

44

"Still. I want you to have time to think about it."

Oh, god. This gorgeous idiot will be the end of me. I grip two handfuls of his white shirt and tug until he looks at me. Until those green eyes bore into mine, like two forest pools I desperately want to swim in.

"I *have* thought about it. So many times, Will."

That flush on his cheeks deepens, and I straighten my spine. Feel a little braver. The heat of his body is *everywhere,* below my thighs, washing over my front, and this feels important, somehow. Like if I don't get through to him now, maybe I never will.

"I thought about it every night I stayed here. Every time we watched a movie together. Every freaking time I *saw* you, Will, I thought about it. What it'd be like to touch your bare skin. How I'd feel with your body on top of mine."

"Crushed?" He smirks, and I hate that self-deprecating tone. I flick his chin.

"Kinda, yeah. In the *best* way. In a way that made me burn up with wanting you."

His throat bobs as he swallows. And I've never seen my best friend like this before—so flayed open and hopeful and raw.

"If we... If we do this, Aubrey, that's it for us. Okay? I can't go back. I need to keep you forever."

Ha. As if that's some kind of terrible warning.

"Maybe I'll keep *you*, Will." I wriggle my hand on his belt, and he takes the hint. Lifts his own away and lets me work the buckle loose. "Did you ever consider that? Maybe I'm possessive. The jealous type."

He chuckles, but he sounds breathless. "Is it weird if I hope so?"

Probably.

45

We're probably crazy. Both messed up about each other, pining in silence for so long and now hurtling at each other at a hundred miles an hour. All I know is, when I tug Will's belt open then move to his shirt, slipping the buttons loose, I feel like I'm unwrapping all my birthday and holiday gifts in one. And when Will frowns at me, serious again, then tugs me down for another deep, probing kiss, my bare, blistered toes curl against the air.

"Shit," he says, when he slips a hand under the hem of my t-shirt. "No panties, Aubrey? You trying to kill me?"

I hum, rocking against the gentle slide of his fingers. "Never kill. Only maim."

It's so different—feeling his fingers there instead of my own. They're bigger and blunter and a bit rougher, but so much better too. And I can feel *everything*, every minute detail of him against my clit, even the little calluses he gets from dealing cards.

"So wet." Will stares at the space between us, where his hand disappears under my hem.

"It's for you," I breathe. *All for you.*

I pick up his other wrist and guide his hand to my breast. He takes over like a champ, kneading me and cupping me and pinching my nipple until I gasp. His hands are so quick and clever—the steady, sure hands of a dealer.

Is this what I pictured with Will? Maybe. I guess I always knew it'd be great. I always knew he'd make me come first before we did anything else; I always knew he'd look at me with worship in those green eyes.

But there are details I didn't predict. The faint hint of cigar smoke clinging to his hair; the way I can feel his heartbeat thudding when I place my palms on his chest.

He crooks his finger and I come in a rush, clenching down on his thick finger, and his thumb swoops over my clit, drawing it out until spots float before my eyes.

"Shit, Aubrey." Will fumbles at his pants button. "That's the best thing I've ever seen."

"Wait." I scramble backward off his lap, as clumsy as a newborn colt. Yeesh. One orgasm from Will and I can barely walk straight.

I haven't even seen the rest of him yet.

"Get up." I kick at his ankle, impatient. "In the bedroom. I want you on top of me."

* * *

"I'm going to flatten you."

"No, you won't." I yank my stolen t-shirt over my head, grinning at the low rumble Will makes, and scramble onto the mattress, lying back in what I *hope* is a seductive pose.

Mostly I just feel breathless. Needy. Like if he doesn't climb on top of me right-freaking-now I'll burst into flames.

Will watches me from the foot of his bed, his intense gaze boring into me. I squeeze my thighs together, shifting restlessly on the covers.

"*Will.*"

His shirt hangs open, the black suspenders still looped over his shoulders and his bow tie dangling loose beneath the collar. Dark hair dusts his broad chest, then runs in a line down the swell of his stomach, disappearing into his black pants.

Will palms the rigid line of his cock, hungry gaze roving over me.

"Will!"

"Alright, alright." He closes his eyes for a second. Pinches the bridge of his nose. And when he looks at me again, it's like something's shifted. His mind's made up. "Are you ready for me?"

"*Yes.*"

He leaves the shirt on. The shirt and the undone bow tie—I think he's forgotten he's even wearing it—but the rest of his clothes go, piling steadily on his bedroom floor. The lights of the city wash through his sheer curtains, painting his big body in red and gold.

I lift my arms as he leans a knee on the mattress. The whole bed dips, tilting toward his weight.

"Are you sure—"

"Will!" I snap. "Oh my god. You are such a freaking tease. If you don't get your ass up here right this second—"

He moves quickly, looming over me and pressing me down into the bed, the open halves of his shirt brushing against my sides. He's warm and soft and hairy and I could *weep* with how perfect he feels. I loop my arms around his neck and yank him closer.

"Don't hold back."

"Aubrey. If I'm not careful, I could snap you like a twig."

"Yeah, now we're talkin'. Say more things like that."

Will shakes his head, then kisses me hard. Lets a little more of his weight settle on me. One end of his bow tie swings forward, brushing against my collarbone.

I wish I could say that because it's Will, it doesn't hurt. But he's as big between the legs as he is everywhere else, and compared to him, he calls me *pocket-size,* so when he finally presses the broad head of his cock inside me, the air punches from my lungs.

"Aubrey?"

Damn. My legs are twitching. The small of my back's suddenly sweaty.

"I'm good," I grit out. "Keep going."

Honestly, it could suck, and I'd make him keep going. I've wanted this too long to turn back now. But as he rocks into me slowly, by turns pushing forward then letting me adjust, the sting of his intrusion fades away, and is replaced by something else.

An ache.

A *delicious* ache.

I bite my lip, then rock up my hips.

"Jesus!" Will surges forward another inch, like he can't help it, spearing me hard to the mattress. Then, strained: "Why are you laughing?"

I gasp for breath through my giggles. "You've got me. I'm harpooned."

It's not funny for long, though. Not once our bodies seal together, nothing between us, not even air, and Will kisses my forehead, my cheek, the tip of my nose.

Not when he starts *moving,* really moving, and that hungry ache spreads hot and liquid through my whole body until I can't think, can't breathe, can't do anything except meet him thrust for thrust, clawing Will's back through his shirt.

He's right. I'm flattened. I couldn't push him off if I tried.

I don't try, but the thought sends another wave of heat roaring through my veins.

The room fills with our ragged breaths. With rumbling noises from Will's chest, and my broken moans. There are other sounds too—the bed frame creaking, practically screaming for mercy, and the wet sound of our flesh slapping together. It should be weird or off-putting, but instead it all pushes me higher. Twists the knot in my belly tighter and tighter until I'm bursting out of my skin.

"I'm going to—oh, *shit*!" I crest the wave and stiffen under Will, shaking and whimpering and flushing red-hot. It goes on and on, wracking my body with tremors, and when Will buries his damp forehead against my shoulder and lets go too, that knocks me into another round of gasping and twitching.

It's sweaty. Ungraceful. Undignified. Moisture pools between my legs, seeping onto Will's sheets in a way that makes me blush.

It's the best thing I've ever done.

"Will." I shake his shoulder gently. He's a dead weight on top of me. "Will. Are you alive?"

My best friend rolls over with a groan, then I'm scooped up and summarily draped across his chest.

Our legs tangle together. My smooth, bare ones against his strong, hairy ones, and I probably shouldn't like that so much.

"When can we do that again?" I ask as soon as I've got my breath back.

Will rumbles a laugh, tossing an arm over his forehead. "You're gonna kill me, Aubrey."

"I am?"

He grins, still half hidden beneath his arm. "Oh, yeah. But what a way to go."

I know *that* feeling. My body's more wrung out than after a double-show day, and already I want to go back for more.

There's time, though.

Plenty of time.

The two of us have all the time in the world.

Will

~~~~~~~~~~⟨⟩~~~~~~~~~~

ne year later

The dressing room hums with chatter as I tap on the door. I always knock—don't want to take anyone by surprise, that's for sure—but the girls are used to me by now. More importantly, they know that I only have eyes for my wife.

Sure enough, when someone calls out for me to enter, I step through and the second I spot Aubrey, I've got tunnel vision. We could be alone on a silent street, for all that I notice anyone else. The rest of the room is a blur of color and noise, and my gaze is fixed on Aubrey where she smiles at me in her mirror.

Her red hair's piled high for the show, sprayed into a bouffant. She hates it, but I think she looks gorgeous. Like one of those classic pin up models, especially with her beauty spot and cherry red pout.

"Did you finish early for the night?" Aubrey doesn't raise her voice, but it cuts through everything else, sweet and clear. I nod, stepping forward with both hands shoved in my pockets.

My thumb brushes against the corner of my gift for her. The thick wedge of hundred dollar bills; a tiny portion of the frankly insane tip I got from a big winner tonight.

It's huge. The biggest tip I've ever received.

It could change our lives, and I'm giving it to my wife. We can do whatever she wants—travel around the world, move to a bigger place, save it for our first baby. Anything.

"Good show?" My voice is rough. My throat's been tight since I stuffed this money in my pocket, since I realized what I can give Aubrey now. It's not as much as she deserves—no amount could ever be that much—but it's something.

Lord, it's something.

"Pretty good." She nods wryly at the vase of white roses on her table. "Someone in the audience liked it, anyway."

The old jealousy twists in my chest, but I push it down, same as always. My wife is a beautiful woman, and there will *always* be men who covet her, especially when she dances so perfectly every night.

I trust her, though. That's all that matters. And burlesque makes her happy, so I'd never make her feel bad about it.

"I've got a surprise for you." I rub my thumb along the stack of bills again.

Aubrey's eyebrow twitches up in the mirror. The last time I had a *surprise* for her, she ended up tied to our bed frame for hours, blindfolded and begging.

The tip of her pink tongue darts out. Wets her bottom lip. "I'm nearly done here," she murmurs, cheeks flushing.

"Good."

Maybe I'll do something like that again first. Work her over until she's loose-limbed and satisfied; until she's got that happy, glazed look in her eye. Then tell her about the tip when she's all loved up and breathless.

So many possibilities. I stand behind Aubrey's chair, watching her remove her makeup in the mirror, and it's like the future yawns open in front of us, big and exciting.

"Aubrey?"

"Hm?" She glances up from blotting her lipstick, smiling softly when she meets my eyes.

"I love you."

Her smile deepens. Brings out her dimples. "I love you too."

Sapphire makes a gagging noise next to us, but we're both too busy staring at each other to respond.

The money's heavy in my pocket.

My wife winks at me in the mirror.

Yeah. Life is good.

||

Big Bratva

Description

She's dropped on my doorstep with a burlap sack on her head.

The diplomat's daughter. The one they're all looking for.

Keep her safe. That's what my brother tells me. Not because he cares for the girl, but because she's his leverage. His ticket to the big time.

I got myself out of this city's underworld over a year ago, and with one knock on my door, I'm dragged right back in.

I should tell him no. Should toss her out on the street. But the second I lay eyes on her, something inside me screams that she's mine to protect.

It's nonsense, of course. I can't let her get close. Sweet,

innocent girls like her have no business with brutes like me.

I'll hold her for a few days; I'll get my brother his big break.

Then I'll forget she was ever here.

Ilya

I'm uncorking a bottle of wine when someone pounds on the door. It's not a polite knock; not a neighbor's gentle tap. It's a thumping fist, one that rattles the front door in its frame and drowns out the soft strains of classical music I have playing.

I sigh. Place my wine bottle, still corked, but now stabbed through with a corkscrew, on the marble kitchen island, and pinch the bridge of my nose.

Nothing good ever came from someone pounding on my door. Not in my whole life.

"Ilya!" a deep voice calls, and I suppose I should be relieved to recognize my brother.

I'm not.

"Ilya, open your fucking door."

Charming. Perhaps I should leave him out there, emergency and all. Perhaps I should finish opening my wine, then relax with a glass or two for the evening as I had planned, listening to music and reading a book.

The fist pounds on my door again. My *brother's* fist. That asshole will draw attention to me; his racket will make my neighbors ask questions.

My steps are slow but steady through my apartment, my leather dress shoes creaking and sweat prickling on the palms of my hands. It's not that I don't trust my brother, per se. It's that I trust him to be exactly as he always is: a viper.

He knows when I've reached the door. He must hear me coming, or see my shadow play across the floor, because he stops pounding and yelling, finally.

Good. I can't afford any extra attention. My situation is precarious enough as it is.

I wipe the palms of my clammy hands on the front of my dress shirt. Then flip the lock, and pull my front door wide.

"Idiot," Vasily hisses, barging inside, dragging a person with a burlap sack on their head by the elbow. It's a woman, I realize with a lurch, a slip of a thing in a gray dress. Unmistakable, even with her face hidden. "You left us out there for too long. We could have been seen."

"Maybe if you'd knocked quietly, you'd have drawn less attention." I frown at Vasily's captive. She's silent, trembling, her wrists bound and her fingers knotted together. "And maybe I'd have been more inclined to answer the door."

Vasily snarls, and my back stiffens. It's always been like this with him, even when we were boys. I always knew, somewhere deep in my hind brain, that he'd kill me without a flicker of emotion if he ever thought me no longer useful.

When I left the bratva a year ago, taking great pains to extricate myself, I knew there was a high chance of a sharp blade in the night. If not from them, from *him*. I'm less useful to my brother these days.

Or I thought I was.

"What do you want, Vasily?"

I don't do this shit. Captives. Young women. I *never* did, and I'm sure as hell not starting now. I was always the money guy, a fixer, greasing palms and working the business scene. Vasily used to goad me for it, saying I was afraid to get my hands dirty.

Well, and what if I was? As if not wanting to commit violence is a personality flaw.

Such a waste, he'd always mutter, prodding at my bicep. Okay, so I look the part of a bruiser. Vasily wanted me to be an enforcer when he first got us into the organization–me a wide-eyed fifteen year old, him two years my senior.

They knew with one look at me, I didn't have the stomach for it. I still don't. So why the hell is there a kidnapped woman standing in my hallway?

"I need to lay low."

My scoff is loud. Vasily *always* needs to lay low. He's always pissing someone off, ruffling powerful feathers. He calls me an idiot, but he's the one with a death wish.

"Then take her with you."

The woman in the hood clenches her fingers together tighter, the knuckles paling to the color of bone, and for a ridiculous moment, I regret that command. I want to keep her here. Give her a glass of wine and let her relax with a book, too.

It's nonsense. She wouldn't be a guest, she'd be a captive, and sure enough Vasily shoves her toward me, her ankle boots scuffing over the floorboards. I reach out to steady her but she catches herself before she falls, and I'm left with an outstretched arm, hovering uselessly in the air.

"You know who she is?" He's grinning. So pleased with

himself. "Take off the hood. Then tell me I should take her with me."

Foreboding pools in my gut, sickly and heavy. I pinch the scratchy burlap sack between finger and thumb, and tug it gently off his captive's head.

Mussed blonde hair–shoulder length and so pale it's nearly white.

Wide, watery blue eyes, terrified and darting.

A gray gag that cuts into a pretty pink mouth, and a freckled nose that flares with each panicked breath.

It's a one-two punch in my chest. First: she's so fucking beautiful. Second: she's the one from the news. The one they're all looking for: the diplomat's daughter. Snatched on the way home from her evening class last night, with the whole city in uproar searching for her.

Well. The police won't be searching *too* hard, not if this is bratva business. Not if they know what's good for them.

Fuck. Poor thing. She probably doesn't even know yet how screwed she really is.

"The Rochdale girl."

Vasily nods, beaming. He spreads his arms like a magician presenting his latest trick, and as I stare at my brother's pointed features, I feel sick.

"Grabbed her myself. What a catch, eh, brother?"

A *catch*. I swallow down bile. Taking a deep breath, I turn back to the girl, scanning her for signs of injury. There's a small cut above one eyebrow, and her dress is rumpled but not torn or stained.

"Did you hurt her?" I grate out.

"No." Vasily snorts. "I'm not an idiot. This girl is my ticket to the big time."

Right. Because that's the only reason for restraint that would make sense to my brother. I rub my temples, head aching. How is this my life? How did I get here?

"You…"

You can't leave her here. That's what I was about to say. Because I worked so fucking hard to get out of this life, and I nearly got killed a dozen times in the process. But get out I did, and now my wretch of a brother wants to drag me back in, kicking and screaming. All for his ticket to the big time.

I know, without question, he wouldn't do the same for me. He'd stab me in the back sooner than help me. But what's his alternative? Or rather—what's *her* alternative? Vasily's problems, I can't bring myself to care about, but the Rochdale girl?

He might not have hurt her yet. But if she stays with him for a long time, there are no guarantees. If anything, it'd be tempting fate.

"This job." I stare at her as I talk. She gazes up at me, glassy eyed with terror. Like a deer caught in headlights on the road. "What's your endgame? Does she die?"

Vasily rubs the dark scruff on his jaw. The sleeve of his black coat pulls up at the motion, revealing an expensive watch and the jagged edges of a tattoo. "Not if it goes to plan."

"And the plan is?" My words are sharp with impatience. And Vasily bristles, but he doesn't try anything. Not here in the light of the hallway, where we're squared up to each other. A fair fight.

Vasily may be older, more vicious, but he's half my size. Slim and angular, and only a few inches taller than the woman he snatched off the street.

I could crush him in one fist, if I felt so inclined. I'm pretty

63

sure that's the only thing that's kept me alive all these years.

"A deal with her father. His daughter's safety in return for his future cooperation." Vasily inhales deeply, and his eyes go dreamy. "You know what a coup this would be, Ilya? Landing a big fish like that for the bosses?"

Sure. Like Vasily said.

She's his ticket to the big time.

And it makes no sense that he'd kill her—it'd undo all his work. That's the only reason I agree.

Wide blue eyes watch me as I dip my head, scratching my chin.

"Alright, brother. Leave her with me."

Madison

From one brutal stranger to another, I'm passed over like a parcel, and the slam of the door behind me makes me flinch. This guy's way bigger than the last one, a tower of muscle and bone, and his slate gray eyes are irritated. Weary.

He's dressed more like a businessman than a mobster. I don't relax, though. I don't think I'll ever let my guard down again.

God, I was so stupid. Skipping the tram and walking home instead, because the stars were so *pretty* and my painting class was so *fun,* and nothing bad could ever happen to me on a crowded city street, right?

Wrong. That asshole bundled me into his car right under a streetlamp, and no one even glanced over. No one even *cared.*

"Are you injured?"

The man spoke in rapid Russian with my captor, too fast for me to catch more than half of their words, but now he speaks in—slightly slower—English. He moves forward a step, and I stumble back until my shoulders hit the door.

Something like shame flickers over the man's face. His strong jaw tightens, a muscle leaping in his temple.

Hey, I don't care if this isn't fun for him. He's still doing it, isn't he? So as far as I'm concerned, he can jump off a bridge.

"I have bandages. Painkillers." The man gusts out an exhausted sigh. "If you need them."

I jerk my head from side to side. Even if my leg was dangling off, I wouldn't want him to touch me.

"Alright," the man says, then gently takes my elbow. "Alright. Come with me."

He leads me through a luxurious open plan apartment. Classical music plays softly in the kitchen; the scent of fancy cooking floats in the air. Everything is polished wood and bronze and sumptuous fabrics. Like a wealthy professor lives here, not a criminal.

Through the large glass windows, the city lights wink and glitter, spreading out below for miles. It's nighttime, then. With the burlap hood and the hours locked in the trunk of that creep's car, I wasn't sure.

"Are you hungry?" he asks, his voice deep. Gentle. He sounds surprised by his own question, like it only just occurred to him.

I shake my head at the same time as my stomach growls loud enough to shake the walls. The man huffs a quiet laugh and changes direction, steering us back toward the kitchen.

"I want to feed you," he tells me. "I'd much rather make you comfortable while you're here. But if I remove the gag and you scream–there will be nothing for it. You'll have to go hungry."

I shrug, letting him tow me into his cavernous kitchen. Spotlights shine from the ceiling, and he pulls a stool up to a large island counter top. There's an abandoned bottle of wine, half uncorked on the counter, and I snort, settling onto the stool. I'm glad both of our plans have been ruined tonight.

He follows my gaze, then his mouth quirks up in a rueful flicker of a smile. "Would you like a glass?"

I shake my head. There's no way in hell I'll risk getting drunk near this stranger.

He shrugs, echoing my movement. "Suit yourself."

This man… he doesn't *seem* like a mobster. He's nothing like the deranged asshole who brought me here, anyway. There's no undercurrent of violence to his every move like the other guy; no threatening leer when he looks at me. If anything, he just seems… tired.

"Promise you'll be good?" Thick fingers pinch the sides of my gag, and I nod. If the other guy said those words to me, they'd have been mocking. Meant to make me feel small. But the way *this* man says them, it's steeped in irony. Like he's making fun of himself.

I don't know what to make of my new captor.

He's gentle as he pulls the gag from between my teeth, lifting the strip of fabric over my head. And… ew.

It's grubby. Disgusting. The man's nose wrinkles as he studies it, then he tosses it to the counter top with a sigh.

"Please don't make me put that in your mouth again. Or at least give me time to wash it first."

My lips twitch, but I force the smile away.

No. I will not like the man holding me captive.

"I made lamb tonight." He tilts his head toward the oven, but I don't look there. I'm too busy studying *him*. He's got short dark hair, threaded with gray at the temples, and his five o'clock shadow has a silvery sheen. Deep lines score the corners of his eyes, but for all that, he doesn't look more than forty.

Just a very exhausted forty.

At this rate, I'll probably age extra fast too—if I get to age at all.

It's a sobering thought, and I miss the other options he gives me. Too busy picturing my parents receiving the news of my death.

Would they cry in private? Or only for the cameras?

"Lamb, please," I rasp once the man finishes his menu recital. He nods once, then turns to dig a plate out of a cupboard.

This is it. I could make a dash for the door—could yell for his neighbors and sprint for the stairwell. But he knows this building far better than I do. I don't even know what floor we're on. And yelling for help didn't save me last night, did it?

Eat, then scream, I decide as the scent of roasted lamb washes over me. Saliva fills my mouth, and I stare dry-eyed as he fills my plate with meat and vegetables, then pours over a thick brown gravy. This way, I get a meal before I'm gagged again. And to that end...

I clear my aching throat. "Could I have a glass of water, please, sir?"

Always be polite with your captor. That feels like self-preservation 101. But the man jolts, glancing back at me like he's shocked I spoke at all, never mind so politely.

"Of-of course. Forgive me."

No, I don't think I will, I muse as he sets a plate of warm food in front of me with a fork, then goes to fetch me a drink.

He doesn't offer to untie my hands.

I don't ask.

* * *

This man seems to feel almost as awkward as I do. It's like he's never held a girl captive before. After I've eaten and downed two full glasses of water, he sets the dishes next to the sink then turns and stares at me, eyebrows pinched in a frown.

"Where did Vasily keep you overnight?" he asks, like I hold the cheat codes to this whole endeavor.

I raise an eyebrow. "In the trunk of his car."

"Fuck." The man scrubs a palm over his face, his stubble crackling. Yeah, something told me he wouldn't go for that. You don't feed a girl lamb then stuff her in a trunk. "I'm–I'm not going to do that."

"You don't drive?" I ask lightly, and my captor barks out a surprised laugh.

"I do. But there are boxes in my trunk."

I hum. "Inconvenient, then."

God, what is this? What are we doing? We're standing here in his kitchen, teasing each other like old friends, and meanwhile my hands are bound and I don't even know his name. I knot my fingers together and squeeze until the bones ache.

I can't relax here. Not even when something about this man sets me instinctively at ease.

He knew the asshole who snatched me off the street. This is some good cop, bad cop nonsense.

"Would you… would you like to use the bathroom? You can relieve yourself, take a shower, have fresh clothes…"

Oh, god. A *shower.* It may have only been one day and night since I was snatched, but I feel grimier than after a week of camping. My skin is sticky with dried sweat, and my sweater dress reeks. I'm like the walking embodiment of that filthy gag.

Not to mention those two full glasses of water. If I don't pee soon, I'll start dancing on the spot.

But...

"Alone?"

He winces but nods. Like he hates that I even had to ask. "Of course."

He still nips into the bathroom first–takes out his razor and checks for other potential weapons. Then places a towel, a new toothbrush, and a stack of men's clothing on my bound hands with an apologetic expression.

I open my mouth to ask, but quick as a flash, his hands snake beneath the pile to my wrists.

I don't even realize he's untied me until I see the grimy bonds hanging from his grip.

Ilya

The Rochdale girl emerges from the master bathroom in a cloud of scented steam. She smells like my soap and shampoo. Citrus and sandalwood. Over in the kitchen, the sound audible through the walls, the washing machine rumbles as it washes her clothes.

A possessive thrill snakes through my gut.

She's in my home.

She smells like me.

"Better?" I don't turn away from the window, watching her reflection in the dark glass instead. The girl hums, stepping around the edge of my bed and squeezing the ends of her damp hair with the towel. She's dwarfed by the clothes I gave her–a pair of navy checked pajama bottoms and a plain white t-shirt. Her bare toes poke out beneath the pooled hems of my pants.

She glances at the doorway, lips pursed, considering. She's weighing the risks of making a run for it, and I don't blame her. How could I? Especially since she's no longer bound and gagged. Her chances are as good now as ever.

"The door is locked," I say softly, hating every word. "I have the only key." She glances past me to the balcony next, her chin resolute. "We're twenty-three floors up," I add.

Watching her shoulders slump, I feel like a monster. Fuck, I don't want to trap her here. I don't want any part of this–none except keeping her safe.

"What would happen if I screamed?" She asks it casually. Like I've presented her with a puzzle to solve, and she wants to clarify the rules. "Would the neighbors care?"

I doubt that she'll trust my answer, but I give her the truth anyway. "One neighbor is an elderly woman. Quite deaf. And on the other side... a bratva informant."

"Reporting to you?"

"Spying on me," I correct.

She frowns, but she doesn't ask me to explain. And I'm oddly disappointed by that, by her lack of interest in me, but once again–I cannot blame her. Why should she care that I'm as trapped in this moment as she is? I'm the one holding the door key.

"I've never..." she trails off, stirring the air by the hem of her t-shirt like she's searching for words. "I've never been kidnapped before. What happens next?"

I shrug, equally lost. "I suppose I keep you safe and fed and warm until your father agrees to Vasily's demands."

She swallows, the movement visible in the dark glass. Why can't I turn and face her?

Well.

I know why.

"And if he doesn't agree?"

A stone sinks through my belly. I know what she's ask-ing–will Vasily kill her if his plan falls through? Most likely, if he gets his way. But Vasily's not the one looking after her. I am.

"I'll see you safely home," I tell her, turning at last so she can see I mean it. Fuck Vasily. Fuck everything about this. Even if I need to disappear, to take on a new identity and flee to the other side of the world, I'll do what it takes to keep her safe. I can't live with myself otherwise. "Don't worry about my brother."

She scoffs, but her shoulders are less tense, too. Part of her believes me, and that warms my chest. "So, what? I'm on a forced vacation?"

My lips twitch. "If you like."

I certainly like that idea. Nothing would please me more than bringing her whatever books or films she desires. Perhaps playing chess with her, or cooking together.

Whiling away the next few days with this young woman will hardly be a hardship. Except for the elephant in the room, of course.

"What is your name?" I can hardly keep thinking of her as *the Rochdale girl*.

"Madison," she whispers.

Madison. So all-American. So out of place, here in the heart of bratva territory.

"What's yours?"

I blink. "Ilya."

Fuck. Should I have told her that? It's a common enough name, but it can hardly be a smart thing for a captor to share. Along with my brother's name, and the view from that window...

I suppose I'll be uprooting soon anyway.

It's a shame, because I *like* this apartment. It's the first thing in my life that's been mine, all mine, untainted by the grim realities of the world. A safe haven... until now, anyway.

But Madison is not a taint on my home. As she drifts across the rug to peer at the books stacked on my chest of drawers, she looks ethereal in the moonlight. Like a princess in baggy pajama pants.

"I guess I should go to sleep." Madison pokes at the spine of the top book. The title is in Russian, but she tilts her head to read it. "It wasn't exactly a five star experience in the trunk of your brother's car."

No. I expect not. And at the reminder of how Vasily treated her, a wave of anger coasts up my spine, hot and urgent, tensing my back and making my heart pound.

My hands ball into fists. My teeth grind. He will never—*never*—touch Madison again. If he does, I'll tear him limb from limb.

Madison glances at me, eyebrows raised. I blow out a breath and force my hands to relax. "Where should I sleep, Ilya?"

"In here," I say before I really think.

Because it's my bed. It's *obviously* my bed, with my book and reading glasses on the nightstand, the closet filled with my clothes, while there's a perfectly usable guest room down the hall. I could put her in there, no problem, but I'm hit with the primal urge to get her scent on my sheets.

I'll sleep on the living room sofa. I need to make sure she doesn't sneak out, anyway.

"In here," Madison repeats, an odd expression on her face. Like she heard all my rapid fire thoughts, blaring at her like a siren.

"Yes." I'm gruff now. Embarrassed. "Get some sleep. And don't try anything, or I'll have to retie your hands."

More unwanted heat crackles through my body at the thought.

God, I'm depraved.

* * *

"Everything good?" Vasily's voice is gleeful in my ear. I squeeze the phone, irritation closing my throat, and stare at my closed bedroom door.

Four hours, it's been. Four hours, and somewhere in that period, I lost the last remaining loyalty I ever felt for my brother. My only priority now is getting Madison home safely. And keeping myself alive, too, if I can.

At the moment, the best way to achieve that is to go along with Vasily's scheme. But the second that changes, I'm taking her away from here. It won't occur to him that he'll need to stop me.

"It's fine," I clip out. "She's safe. Not hurt."

He won't care about that, but I want it on the record. Madison is safe with me, damn it.

"Keep an eye on her." Vasily's breaths are heavy. Labored. It's all the excitement of his *catch*. "She's a wildcat. Nearly scratched out my eyes when I pushed her into my car."

Pride swells my chest. Pride I have no business feeling.

I hope Madison got a few good knocks in. I hope she kicked him square in the balls.

"I'll watch her." As if I could look away. She's the kind of beautiful that's hard for your brain to comprehend. Like dawn breaking over the city. Like the stars.

"She's my ticket to the big time," Vasily says for the millionth time, and god, if I hear that phrase one more time, I'll bite through my tongue.

"So you've said."

"Don't fuck this up for me, brother."

"Of course I won't."

I hang up with a sour taste in my mouth. Vasily thinks I'm meek. Biddable. And I suppose I have been at times, especially when we were growing up and he was the only family I knew. Then after, as bratva, the options were stark: obey or die. I kept more honor than Vasily, but I also wanted to live.

I frown at the bedroom door like I could see her through the wood. Madison, small and waif-like, asleep in my bed with her icy blonde hair splayed over my pillow.

Vasily had better watch his step.

I won't obey him in this. Not when it comes to her.

Madison

Ilya is a snorer. I shouldn't be surprised–he's a mountain of a man, a craggy cliff face, and his lungs must be bigger than a set of bellows inside that rib cage. So I shouldn't be surprised, and I *definitely* shouldn't find it endearing.

It's useful. That's all that matters.

It tells me now is my chance to escape.

The living room is dark when I nudge the bedroom door open, moving painfully slowly so the hinges don't creak. My bare feet are cold against the floorboards, and I shiver in my borrowed t-shirt, my nipples pebbling against the fabric.

It's not ideal. If I run out into the street like this, I'll lose half my toes to frostbite before I find help, but desperate situations call for desperate measures.

There's only one apartment key–that's what Ilya said earlier. Only one key, and he has it. I tiptoe up to his sleeping body, slumped sideways on the sofa, like he was trying to sit up and stay awake.

Well. It must be tiring, holding a girl captive. Very bad for the nerves.

My fingers tingle when I glance at his pants pockets. They're bulging slightly, like he's got stuff in there. A wallet, maybe. A phone. They're the first place I should look, but they're so dangerously close to those strong thighs.

I breathe in steadily through my nose, then exhale through pursed lips.

Focus.

This is it. I'm getting out. It doesn't matter how *sweet* my captor pretends to be—I'm blowing this joint.

On an impulse, I reach out a shaking hand. With one fingertip, I tease his shirt collar away from his throat.

There. I knew it. A key hangs around his neck, resting against the muscled swell of his chest. I bite my lip as I lean over the sofa, fiddling with the knotted cord and ordering myself to stop noticing Ilya's chest hair. Stop breathing in deep lungfuls of his masculine scent.

My captor grunts in his sleep. He shifts slightly, eyebrows pinching in a frown, and I hover over the sofa, a nervous statue.

Then the snores start again, and relieved, I return to the knot.

It's so easy. That's the weirdest part. With the moonlight and Ilya's snores and the misplaced certainty in my stomach that if he caught me, he wouldn't hurt me—none of it feels quite real. It's like a children's game, something we might have played in the schoolyard, and as I race through Ilya's apartment a few minutes later with the key clutched in my hand, I'm actually grinning.

That thrill melts away once I'm out of his apartment, sprinting down his building's corridor. I skip a few doors—maybe he was lying, but maybe his neighbors really are useless—then start knocking, hand shaking with adrenaline.

No one answers the first door.

Nor the second.

I curse and move on, knuckles stinging from pounding on wood. What if no one comes? I'll have to run into the street dressed like this. It'd be like hanging an 'I'm vulnerable!' sign around my neck.

The third door wrenches open under my fist. A sour-faced woman with curlers in her hair opens her mouth to yell at me, then does a double-take, stepping back. I see the exact moment she recognizes me from the news. There's even a flicker of pity.

Then the door slams in my face.

It's the same at the next two apartments. I guess the word's out—the bratva took the diplomat's daughter. No one defies the bratva, not if they want to live.

"Please," I yell in my clumsy Russian, banging hard on the sixth door. My voice is hoarse, though it's the first word I've said in hours. I glance down the corridor, but there are no footsteps yet. No bellow of outrage from Ilya. "Please help me."

The door flies open, and a young man stares at me. He looks a few years older than me, mid-twenties maybe, with ashy brown hair and a loose gray sweater under a zip up hoodie.

"Please," I mumble. The young man's eyebrows lower. He grabs my elbow and starts to tug me through his door. But I know as soon as his fingers close around my arm, I've made a mistake; this man is no savior.

This is not the gentle way Ilya touched me. This man aims to bruise.

"Stop!" I kick out, my teeth clacking together as I buck and fight. God, how many evil men are going to grab me this week? Some dazed, horrified part of me wants to laugh.

No one can truly be this unlucky. No one.

"Bitch," the man grinds out, yanking harder on my arm, and I howl, fighting harder. *No.* No, no, no.

I don't hear Ilya coming. All I know is a rushing noise past my ear, and the sickening crunch of bone, and then the man's grip on me loosens as he crumples into a pile in his doorway.

Ilya stares down at his neighbor, knocked out cold with one blow. His chest heaves beneath his dress shirt, but his face is blank. Impassive as stone. And he doesn't look at me as he mutters, "Let's go."

I don't argue. I'm ashamed to say that I don't even fight as he leads me down the corridor back to his apartment, my trembling fingers clutching at his sleeve.

* * *

"That was very foolish." Ilya mirrors my wince as he dabs a wet cloth against the cut on my forehead. It's the cut his brother gave me, reopened by his creepy neighbor, and this is probably the last man on earth I should let tend it, his own bloody knuckles gripping the white cloth. "If I hadn't woken up and found you gone, what then?"

What then, indeed. I'm putting a whole lot of effort into *not* asking myself that question, hunched on the edge of Ilya's bathtub as he kneels before me. My borrowed pajama pants pool around my bare feet, and my toes scrunch against the cold tiles.

Ilya looks even more tired than before he fell asleep. I wet my bottom lip, and his exhausted gaze tracks the movement.

"I'm not sorry."

"No." His mouth quirks; the lines at the corners of his eyes deepen. "I don't suppose you are."

There it is. That calm acceptance I *knew* he'd show me. Somewhere deep down, I knew when I stole the key and crept away that this man wouldn't hurt me. If anything, he just seems impressed that I tried.

Impressed and exasperated. I kick my heels against the edge of the bathtub, feeling more like a teenager caught sneaking out to attend a party than a captive who made a bid for freedom.

"Hey. Don't dent my bathtub."

I snort, tilting my head to give Ilya a better angle. He's got one of those fancy claw foot bathtubs: sturdy and classic, just like its owner. I could push it off the balcony, and it probably wouldn't dent.

"What should I do next time?" Ilya grunts, so I elaborate. "On my next escape attempt. What would you recommend?"

Hey, he gave me insider info about the neighbors. Why not again? But he rolls his eyes and doesn't answer, and god, I don't know why I'm drawn to teasing him like this. Why I so desperately want to hear more of his deep voice, chiding me with ill-concealed admiration.

"There won't be a next time."

"That's what *you* think."

"Don't make me bind your hands again," he warns, stonier now. I bite my lip, staring at his craggy face, so close to mine. My fingers are knotted loosely in my lap.

"You wouldn't."

His frown deepens. "I would."

And finally, *finally*, a shiver prickles over my skin. It's the reminder I've been looking for–the instinct that tells me to be careful. To be wary of this man. His brother snatched me off the *street*; he knocked that man unconscious with a single, brutal punch.

But the tingle of fear doesn't last, because Ilya sighs, his huge shoulders slumping.

"I swore to keep you safe, Madison." *Dab. Dab.* The cloth patting my forehead is so gentle. As soft as his faint accent. "I'll bind your hands again if that's the only way. I'll do whatever it takes, even if it makes you hate me."

God, why do I believe him?

"I already hate you," I tell him, but there's no heat behind it. No ring of truth. He's keeping me here, yes, but Ilya doesn't *feel* like a captor. Not really. He feels more like what he claims to be–a protector. And maybe it's crazy, but I actually feel bad when he winces, his pale eyes unaccountably sad.

"That's reasonable."

"Uh-huh. Sure is." I kick the bathtub again, my stomach twisted up like a pretzel. And when he rocks back on his heels, getting ready to stand, I grab his wrist without thinking. "Wait. Your turn."

His wrist is so massive in the circle of my fingers. Warm and dusted with dark hairs, his pulse thudding rapidly against my thumb. Ilya's wrist is a *structure*, a feat of big-boned engineering, and when I flip his hand over and take the cloth, his arm is heavy in my grip.

Square knuckles. Big nails, trimmed short. Pale white scars, so faded that I never noticed them before. Ilya doesn't wince when I press the cloth against his torn skin. He doesn't move at *all*, turned to stone on his bathroom floor.

"Thank you for hitting that man," I murmur, the words

so quiet in this silent bathroom. It's just our soft breaths, bouncing off the tiled walls, and the rustle of the cloth. "You got him really good. He went out like a light, like *poof.* Just like that–crumpled on the floor."

Studying his hand like this, I can't help imagining what it would be like if he touched me. Dragged his warm, dry palm over my skin; gripped me in his stern, strong grip. But Ilya grunts, and when I glance at him, he looks kind of uncomfortable.

"I don't like hitting people," he says after a long stretch of me staring at him, willing him to speak. And... what the hell?

I huff a laugh. "Worst captor *ever.*"

Ilya's relieved smile is brighter than the golden glow from the wall sconces. And before I know it, I'm smiling back, cheeks aching, and I don't stop until he pushes to his feet, knees cracking. Then, when he turns his back and leaves me to wash up, my burst of happiness fades.

It's Stockholm Syndrome. Misplaced gratitude for saving me from that guy.

This man is dangerous, and he's holding me against my will.

I'd be a fool to let down my guard.

Ilya

～⚬⚬～

Taking Madison to my bedroom for the second time in one night–that's torture. A special kind of torment, especially with the warmth of her skin bleeding through her borrowed t-shirt against my hand. I steer her gently, one palm splayed over her shoulder blades, and just that small point of contact is enough to make my heart thud.

She *touched* me in the bathroom. Willingly. She tended to my busted knuckles, dabbing at me gently with that cloth like she–like she cared.

Fuck. I don't deserve a single nice thought from this girl. This is a disaster.

"Are you going to behave, or should I tie you to the bed frame?" I say, and I'm trying to tease her about escaping, but as soon as the words leave my mouth, I grimace. They sound heated. Undeniably sexual. No doubt they sound *vile,* coming from a man like me, and I wish I could stuff them back in my mouth. Chew them up and swallow.

Madison eyes me over her shoulder, and her expression is

unreadable. "No. I'm done escaping for one night."

"Good," I rasp, desperate to change the subject. Shit, I never meant to make her uncomfortable. "I'm tired, too."

I'm trying to cover my blunder. Trying to tell her, buried under other words, that she can trust me. I won't come into the bedroom; won't cross those kinds of lines.

Does she believe me? I can't read her little frown.

I've already retrieved the apartment key from Madison's thieving hands. It's not on a cord around my neck any more–I hid it under the fruit bowl in the kitchen while she used the bathroom before bed. There's no guarantee she won't find it again, I suppose, but I can't help wanting to trust her. To believe this fragile truce, even if it only lasts one night.

Still. "If you do escape," I can't help telling her, "wear shoes this time. I put yours away in the hallway cupboard. And take a winter coat, and money from the bureau."

"More top tips from Ilya." Madison smirks at me, flipping back the bed covers and crawling onto the mattress. "I'm learning so much." Her tone is light, but her eyes are hard.

I tug the blankets up to her chin, gut twisting.

What I wouldn't give to do this in real life. To tuck Madison into my bed as a–a *willing* visitor. To climb in next to her and tug her close, pillowing her pretty cheek on my chest.

To roll on top of her and feel her little body arch against mine.

"Sleep well," I say, suddenly desperate to leave, and without thinking, I duck down and press a kiss against her forehead. Madison freezes beneath me, her breaths shallow, and when I straighten up, she stares up at me, eyes wide.

"Forgive me." I charge toward the doorway, ears ringing; I bounce off the fucking chest of drawers before I make it out of the bedroom.

"Goodnight," Madison calls after me, her soft voice strained before the door clicks shut, locking her safely away.

Maybe it's better if she escapes after all. I can't be trusted around this girl, not at all.

* * *

"Cut off a finger." Shortly after dawn, Vasily's voice in my ear stops my breath. I squeeze the phone tight, ice sliding through my veins, staring blindly at the sun rising over the city rooftops.

"That's... extreme."

Vasily snorts. "It's just a finger, brother. Take a pinkie if you want to be a pussy about it, but make sure it's clearly hers. Send it to the embassy with a runner. The diplomat needs more incentive."

I swallow, throat thick. This nightmare only gets worse. "He's not budging?"

"No." Vasily huffs, static crackling down the line. "He's a *patriot*."

He spits the word like a curse, and in this case, I'd have to agree. What kind of man cares more about his career than his own daughter? But of course, that's not my brother's complaint. He's just annoyed his leverage isn't working properly. If he bragged about it to the bosses already, they'll expect results—his neck will be on the line.

"Can you do it?" Vasily's voice is rough with impatience. "Or should I come by the apartment?"

"I'll do it." The words trip out in a rush. "Don't come here. It's suspicious."

Vasily grunts.

Out in the hallway, my bedroom door cracks open. Madison pads into the living room, bleary and sleep-rumpled, and I stare at her with wide eyes, raising a finger to my lips. *Trust me*, I want to beg her, even though I don't deserve it. *Please.*

If Vasily knows I took her gag off–if he suspects I'm too soft–

Madison nods, shoulders straightening and jaw going firm. She's more alert already, and I say nothing as she tiptoes across the rug. Hell, I even lean down a few inches, letting her grip my shoulder for balance as she cranes to listen to the voice floating down the phone, her lips moving as she tries to keep up with the rapid-fire Russian.

"Midnight was the deadline I gave him. After that, I told him we'd send her back in pieces, one day at a time, but the idiot's not playing."

Madison jolts, staring up at me in horror. I shake my head quickly, and she swallows, her blue eyes searching my face.

"So start with a finger," I repeat needlessly. I'm not trying to scare her; I want to catch her up. Make sure she's informed since, you know, it's her body parts on the line. "Why not a chunk of her hair?"

It's a weak counter offer. And sure enough–

"A *finger*," Vasily growls. "We're bratva, not fucking boy scouts, Ilya. We make a threat, we follow through. Can you do it or not?"

Another head shake, just for her. "I can do it."

"Good. Make sure her father gets it by noon. And don't fuck it up, or you're *both* dead."

My brother hangs up, and slowly, I lower the phone. My apartment's never been so silent. So choked with tension.

Madison's staring dead-eyed at the wall, looking smaller than ever in my clothes, and her blonde hair sticks up on one side from finally catching some sleep.

I want to smooth it down. Want to pull her trembling body into my arms. God, I've never wanted to comfort someone more, and yet that was my *brother* on the phone, and I'm in this up to my neck, and why the fuck would she trust me even for a second?

"Families, huh?" Madison's broken laugh makes my chest ache. She's still staring at the wall. "They're the *worst*."

"Yes, they are." I tug her round to face me, heart hammering. "I won't hurt you, sweet girl. I promised, alright? I meant it."

"But your brother said—"

"Fuck my brother." In this moment, I could cheerfully kill Vasily myself. I don't think I'd even blink an eye. "I won't take an—an *eyelash*, Madison."

She wraps her arms around her waist. Holds herself together. And as my breath stutters, she leans forward until her forehead rests against my torso.

My arm hovers in the air, unsure. And when it comes tentatively around her shoulders and she leans heavier against me, I could shout in triumph.

She trusts me. Enough to seek a modicum of comfort, at least; enough that she's not running from the room, screaming for help. It's everything. So much more than I deserve.

"What do we do?" Madison's voice is so small.

I rest the tip of my nose against her hair, breathing her in, and say the words that will change everything.

"We run for our lives."

Madison

After my long stretch of captivity–after sticky, cramped hours of being stuffed in that trunk, so freaking alone; after the cool quiet of Ilya's apartment, his soft music, his softer sheets–the chaos of an inner city train station is like having my ears boxed. It presses on my ear drums and draws my eyes in every direction until I can't focus and everything is a blur.

Ilya's hand wraps around mine, anchoring me. Squeezing tight.

"Stay close." He speaks Russian to me now, so we don't draw attention. Slow enough for me to understand. "Don't make eye contact with anyone."

I nod silently, staring down at my ankle boots. I'm wearing my own gray dress again, but I'm swamped in one of Ilya's sweaters–cream, rolled several times to free my wrists. The sweater nearly reaches the dress hem at my mid thigh, but it can't look any more ridiculous than the old-fashioned flat cap on my head.

Ilya fixed it on me before we left, tucking every strand of my hair under the cap.

"Hide your beauty," he'd murmured to himself, then wrinkled his nose like he didn't think it worked anyways. I've been playing that moment over and over in my head, my stomach fluttering, trying to distract myself from—well, from everything else.

I don't want to lose a finger, damn it. Not even a pinkie. I like all ten of them.

But glancing around the station's crowd now, there are several people wearing flat caps like mine. Guess I blend better than I thought.

Why not the airport? I'd asked in the cab over here, sweat prickling on my palms every time the driver's eyes flicked to me in the rear mirror. But Ilya had barked a command, and the man only stared at the road after that.

Because you'd need ID, he told me, patient as ever. Yeah, duh. *And the bratva has eyes in the airports.*

Jeez. Is there anything the mob doesn't control?

Trains, apparently. Or at least, they're less *interested* in trains, so Ilya thinks this is our best shot to get far away fast–and I guess he'd know. He didn't offer to take me to the embassy and I didn't ask him to. After hearing my father refused to bargain for me… I'm not sure I even want to go home.

Hell, I'm twenty years old. I'm an adult, but I've lived under my father's thumb that whole time, obeying his cold commands and bearing his constant criticism. Maybe this is an opportunity as well as a horror show.

"Stay close," Ilya says again, like he's not gripping my hand tight. I couldn't slip away if I tried, though as he tugs me towards our train, I don't *want* to try.

Something changed this morning, standing together in Ilya's living room. Listening to that phone call, and then hatching a plan for our escape.

We're on the same side now. Team Ilya. Team Madison. Team *us*.

I've never really had someone on my side before. It feels good, in between the waves of terror.

"First class carriage." He steers me there, then holds the train door open as I step inside. Ilya's heavy palm splays over my shoulder blades, guiding me down the aisle past rows and rows of plush, cushioned seats with private tables.

On the rare occasions my family travels on these trains, we always get a private compartment, and I whisper to Ilya, asking why we didn't get one now. I mean, I know he's good for it. I saw all the stacks of cash and the freaking pouch of diamonds he stuffed in that duffel he's got slung over a broad shoulder.

"Hard to blend when there's no one nearby," he murmurs, his words tingling against the shell of my ear. I guess that's true.

We settle in two seemingly random seats. Innocuous, surrounded by other people, just like Ilya said. And he puts me in the window seat, his sweater pooling around me on the cushioned chair, then boxes me in protectively with his bulk.

It's not claustrophobic. Not like the trunk. If anything, when my would-be captor's side presses against mine, I let out a relieved sigh.

"Okay?" His slate gray eyes rake over me, concern etched in every line of his face. He goes to pull his hand away, but I cling tight to his fingers and squeeze.

"Yeah. I'm okay."

There's a pause, then thick fingers wrap more firmly around

mine. Our joined hands settle on my leg, and Ilya's thumb traces back and forth over my knuckles.

Neither of us relaxes until the train draws away, puffing and rattling its way out of the city. I rest my head on Ilya's shoulder and watch as gray streets slowly turn to grassy plains, with snow-capped mountains rising up in the distance.

The sun burns high in the sky, and it's surely past noon by now. I wriggle all ten of my fingers—a little *screw you* to Ilya's brother.

He won't get to hurt me. Not while Ilya's here.

* * *

"Tickets, please."

Hours later, I shrink down behind Ilya's shoulder, watching with one eye as a conductor in a navy blazer clips holes in our paper tickets, idly scanning our faces. He quirks an eyebrow when he sees me, and he doesn't even blink as he hands back the tickets, his gaze lingering on my eyes, my lips, the shape of my body under Ilya's baggy sweater.

"Traveling with your daughter?"

There's something hungry in the conductor's tone. Ilya rumbles a growl.

"With my *wife*."

That does it. The conductor snaps his gaze away, nodding sheepishly at Ilya, and then he's moving away down the aisle, collecting more tickets. I stare at the man beside me, the gentle giant bristling with irritation, and replay his words in my head, over and over in that rough tone.

With my wife.

My wife.

Holy crap. I suck in a shaky breath, wriggling restlessly in my seat.

"Forgive me," Ilya mutters, staring dead ahead.

I huff a laugh. "For what? You were just staking your claim." I meant–I meant for this train ride, for this escape, for the purposes of this ruse, but it sounds like I'm saying something else. Like Ilya really does have a claim over me.

Gray eyes flick to mine, then away.

He doesn't–have a claim. We both know that. But the idea of it isn't... isn't horrible. If anything, it makes warmth spread through my chest until it drips down to my belly. It makes my cheeks heat and my pulse thud faster.

I swallow hard past a dry throat, and god, I can't believe I'm going to do this. It's so risky, but hey, when you're on the run for your life... live a little, right?

I shift our hands against my leg. Slide mine out, then flatten Ilya's palm over my thigh.

Next to me, he stills. His breaths grow harsher.

I've held Ilya's wrist before, and it's familiar as I grip it again. The weight of him, the dark hairs, the toned muscles of his forearm under his shirt. His pulse, tapping extra fast under his skin, racing along to match mine.

The hem of his cream sweater hitches up my legs. My dress, too, as I drag Ilya's hand slowly up the length of my thigh. His fingers twitch, and then he's gripping me, squeezing, playing along too.

Ilya nudges a single fingertip under the hem of my dress.

"Yes," I whisper when he pauses, head cocked. I'm panting already, misting the cool window next to me as grassy fields and farmhouses whip by. "Yes. Please."

Ilya shifts, his seat creaking, and then his hand slides higher.

Disappears under the fabric of my dress. A wide-eyed glance around the train shows only bent heads; newspapers and headphones.

No one's listening. No one's watching.

Something grazes the seam of my leggings. I choke back a squeak.

"Beautiful girl." Ilya's voice is lowered. Gruff. Just for me. He turns and crowds me against the window, so big and broad he blocks out most of the carriage. "Are you bored on this train?"

"Uh-huh." I nod fast, cheeks flushing.

Yes, I'm bored. That's not why I want him, but it is true.

Something touches me there again, sweeping more firmly over the fabric. His thumb, I think.

"And you want to play this game with me? With your big evil captor?"

I snort, and though Ilya doesn't smile, his eyes twinkle. When I nod, my cap scuffs against the chilled glass.

"*Good*," Ilya mutters, and he's so darkly satisfied that I squirm. My hips twitch forward and then he takes the hint, rubbing firmly, *rhythmically*, at the front of my leggings.

Whatever I'd pictured for the first time a man touched me there, it wasn't this–fleeing for our lives on a cross country train, my hair stuffed under a flat cap as a Russian mobster rubs me through the fabric of my clothes. But weirdly, the only thing I'd change is the layers of material between us.

I wish the leggings were gone. My underwear, too.

I wish Ilya was touching me directly, fingers grazing over my heated, slick core.

I tug urgently at his wrist, but he shakes his head once. Too risky, I guess. Or maybe he doesn't want to? But no–Ilya's jaw is clenched hard enough to crack a tooth, and his gaze *burns* as it drags over my body, like he's trying to devour me with his eyes. My nipples harden, prodding at my clothes in answer.

"Later," he grinds out, and I tip my head back with a quiet moan. The vibration of the window rattles my teeth. Later? There'll be a later?

We can do this again?

A slideshow of all the other things we could do together slams into me, one flushed, sweaty image at a time, and more heat pools between my legs. My breath hitches, and I rock my hips forward, rolling against Ilya's circling touch.

It's *good.* So freaking good it sends sparks racing down my limbs, and yet it's still not enough. I need more. I–I need–

Ilya finds my clit, unerring, and pinches it hard through the fabric.

Oh.

I arch in my seat, shuddering and breathless. For a long moment, the rattle and hum of the train fades away, and there's only the roar of blood in my ears. The twitch of my muscles as a deep flush prickles over my skin.

Then I collapse, limbs trembling, and the warmth of Ilya's hand leaves my lap. He turns back to face forward, slapping a newspaper open on his tray table and bowing his head to read.

Um. What?

Blinking, I stare at him, my fevered body cooling under my clothes. It's like the last few minutes never happened. And maybe I'd be pissed at that clear dismissal, maybe I'd turn away and ignore him too, but…

But Ilya's ears are so freaking pink.

I swivel around, sitting straight, and chew on my lip. He didn't *seem* unaffected by what we just did. As waves and waves shuddered through my body, Ilya looked at me with something like awe.

So maybe my mobster is out of his depth too. As surprised by this connection between us as I am.

I nudge his knee with mine. And Ilya gusts out a heavy breath, then shoots me a small smile... and nudges me back.

Ilya

꧁ ꧂

"It's nothing special." I step aside in the hotel room doorway, letting Madison squeeze past and inspect our room. "Nothing that could draw attention."

Our *room*. Singular. There's a good reason—I can protect her much better from inside the same four walls—but I still feel like a dirty old man for wanting this. Madison's sweet company, so close I can smell her; her body stretched out in the same bed. Since feeling her damp heat scorching through her leggings on that train, the rushing in my ears has barely stopped. I'm burning up.

"Still better than your brother's trunk," Madison murmurs, flicking at the ratty bedspread which undulates over a lumpy mattress.

She glances round briefly, and then she's done, blinking back at me with so much trust and expectation. There's not much in this room to inspect—only the sad-looking double bed, two nightstands with lamps, and a wardrobe with crooked doors.

Moth-eaten curtains hang over the window, the glow of

97

street lamps creeping around the edges. We traveled all day to get here, switching trains twice. Trying to throw any pursuers off the scent.

"What's the plan?" Blue eyes watch me, wide and warm.

The plan. Right.

"We should be safe here for a few days, at least. This town's a backwater with a defunct coal mine. There's nothing here for the bratva *or* the Americans to take an interest in."

Madison hums, kicking off her boots and flopping onto the bed in a chorus of wailing bed springs. "And then?"

I swallow. "And then we figure out a way to contact your father. A way the bratva can't intercept."

Her shoulders slump, right before my eyes, but what the hell else am I supposed to offer her? I can't single-handedly take down the bratva, though if anyone could tempt me on that suicide mission, it would be Madison. To make her happy. To keep her safe.

"And then?" She sounds bitter. Madison draws her legs up and rests her chin on her knees.

I frown at her, bemused. "And then you go home."

"Until the next mobster snatches me."

My skin flushes hot at the thought; my fists squeeze until the bones creak.

"That won't happen."

"No?" She glances at me, an eyebrow raised.

"No." It won't. It can't. Just the thought… I wouldn't survive it. "You'll be more careful. Have bodyguards, all that stuff. No more walking home alone at night, yes?"

Those pretty lips press in a hard line. "Way to blame the victim, Ilya. So what, I'm supposed to hide away for my whole life? For as long as my father's career puts me at risk? That could be decades! You think he gives me any kind of say in this?"

I stomp to the wardrobe. Try in vain to fix the crooked doors.

"*Ilya.*"

How did they even break these? It's like they bent the fucking hinges. But she's huffing and puffing behind me, working herself into a stew on the bed, so I make myself answer.

"Maybe," I grit out, though every word tastes foul on my tongue, "you would be safer back home. In America, having your own life. Away from your father."

"Away from *you*?"

Yes.

"No." I slam the wardrobe door again, too hard. Too flustered. "You're safe with me, Madison. I told you."

But my *life* isn't safe. I'm still watched. Still monitored. Still in danger, every day, of being sucked back into the organization I worked so hard to leave. And with a brother like Vasily, dropping bound and gagged girls on my doorstep...

It's not a question of *if*. It's *when*.

How much more freedom do I have left? How many months, weeks, days?

Madison and I have more in common than she thinks. We're both trapped in our circumstances; ham-strung by selfish family members.

"Come with me."

I stare at the scratched wood of the wardrobe, not comprehending. Does she need to leave the room? Find a vending machine or a convenience store?

"We'll get food sent here. Don't worry."

"No, Ilya. You're not listening. Come with me back to

America. We can both find jobs—we could get a place together. My father would never allow me to have my own life like that, but this way, we could *both* escape."

Come with me back to America. The way she says that, soft and beseeching... it's like she really wants it. Like she really wants to keep me with her.

Of course, that desire will not last. After a single day, a single *hour* back in her home country, where she's safe and has options, I will not look so compelling to her. A burly Russian mobster who's twice her age? Ha. I think not.

But leaving with her...

Leaving Vasily and the bratva far behind...

Protecting her across an *ocean*...

Is it possible? Truly?

"I would need a new identity. Perhaps we both would." I'm speaking to the wardrobe still, my voice bouncing off the faded wood, but I know she's listening. Madison's practically holding her breath behind me. "It would take a few days."

"Then take them."

"And we'd need to take a ship, not a plane, to stop the bratva from snatching you again at an airport. The journey across the ocean takes weeks, and is likely not comfortable—"

"I don't care." The bed springs screech, and I turn around to find her kneeling. Reaching for me, cheeks flushed and eyes bright. "This plan is so much better. Come with me, Ilya. Start over with me. *Please.*"

I drift toward her reaching hand like a man in a trance. These words Madison is saying...

"Are you certain?" I croak. "Truly?"

This is—what do they call it? Stockholm Syndrome. That's the only explanation. But perhaps we can do this, we can escape across the world together, and once Madison comes to her senses… I will honor that. I will leave her be.

But I could keep her safe, even then. Watch her from the shadows, protecting my sweet girl. It's an intoxicating image.

Madison nods frantically, her pretty eyes urging me to believe her, so I dip my chin. "Agreed."

And the smile that breaks over her beautiful face–it's like the sun coming out. Peeking through the winter clouds. Her arm stretches further, and then I'm caught, my shirt gripped in her slender fingers.

I let her tug me to the edge of the bed. Place my hands on her waist, my heart slamming hard enough to crack a rib.

She's warm beneath my touch. So small. So full of trust. The memory of the train, her heat, the *noises* she made–they slam into me and I stiffen, jaw clenched.

"Relax," Madison whispers, and she's watching me like she sees me. Like she *knows*. Like the thoughts I have of her–crushed beneath me, arching, *moaning*–are flickering like a movie reel on my forehead. "I want this, too."

She grips my collar on both sides. Raises one eyebrow. Then topples back onto the bed, bringing me down with her.

* * *

The bed shudders over the balding carpet, its wooden frame groaning under our weight. My hands brace on the mattress, a broken spring digging into one palm, but I don't care, not when Madison cranes her neck up and seals her pretty lips to mine.

She's shy. Tentative. So at odds with the confidence of just a few moments ago, my stubbled cheeks scraping against her soft hands as she tilts her head. Explores.

I dip my head with a growl and kiss her back, hard enough that her head drops back against the bed spread. She tastes like the butterscotch toffees she chewed on the train. Gut churning, I kiss her deeper.

Silky blonde hair splays over the frayed fabric. A few strands drift over my fingers in a feather-light touch, and Madison *whimpers*. Sucks on my bottom lip, her body rolling against mine.

Fuck.

I tear my mouth away, panting. "We do not need to do this."

An ankle hooks over my leg, holding me in place. As if *that's* enough to keep a man of my size pinned.

"Well, duh." Madison scowls at me, her cheeks pink. "But I want to. Don't you?"

Yes, of course. I'd trade ten years of my life to keep kissing this girl. But...

"Are you bored again?"

I brace for her answer, but a soft look flickers across her eyes. Empathy. Understanding.

"I'm not bored, Ilya." A single finger snakes under my collar, finding the hollow of my throat. Drawing maddening circles. "I wasn't bored on the train, either. Not really. I *want* you."

I grit my teeth, not ready to accept this just yet. "If you're bored, I can fetch us a pack of cards–"

"Freaking hell! I'm not bored, Ilya!" Madison's eyes flash, and I choke back a groan. Every molecule in my body is screaming at me to flatten her against the bed, to kiss her, *take* her. To turn that scowl into a look of pleading. "Do you really think I'd throw away my first kiss, my first *everything*, because there's nothing better to do?"

First... everything?

I blink. Interesting.

This is the part where if I was a good man, a truly reformed man, I would climb off her. Put some distance between us, breathe in air that's not laced with her scent, and do the right thing. I'd keep my hands far away.

But I'm not a good man; I'm ex-bratva. I fought for every single good thing in my life, and I've known blood. Violence. Fear and pain. So when the most beautiful girl in the world offers up a gift like her first *everything* on a silver platter, I do not climb off her.

No. Far from it.

I lower to my elbows, crushing her to the bed with a groan.

Madison whimpers again, her legs wrapping around my waist. Her cool little hands dip in and out of my shirt, exploring between the buttons, delving under my open collar. Stroking over my chest hair and tracing my collarbone.

"You are a bad girl," I grind out, wedging my hips in the cradle of her thighs.

Madison snorts. "Well, I'm *trying* to be. You're fighting me every step of the way."

Not anymore. No, now, I'm listening to the pulse thudding in my ears. To the heat snaking through my body, making my nerves spark and my hips roll.

I spear her to the bed, my cock jutting behind my suit pants. I line up with the seam of her leggings and I thrust at her, fucking her through layers of fabric.

"This is how you'd take me," I tell her, head dropping to smell her neck. Bite her jaw. Her body rocks across the bed spread with every thrust. "With your legs open wide and your hands clawing at my back, gasping for more."

The flush on Madison's cheeks deepens. Pearly white teeth dig into her bottom lip. When I kiss her again, I slide my tongue into her mouth, showing her with actions as well as words how I'd fuck her. Plundering, merciless.

She doesn't know what she's asking for.

Maybe she has a better idea now.

"Mmph." Madison shifts beneath me, then tilts her head. She sucks on my tongue, and fuck, maybe this is a two-way conversation. A mutual promise.

My hips roll harder, thrusting her higher up the bed. A few layers of fabric, and that's it. It would be so easy to reach down and tear her leggings open at the seam. To draw my cock out and cram myself inside her slick pussy; to hold her hips still and wedge deeper, *deeper*.

My hands shake as I push off her. Madison splutters, starts to complain, but then I'm settling my shoulders between her spread thighs.

We're not done here.

I won't take–won't take *that* from her, but there are other gifts I could steal.

Madison lifts her hips as I draw her leggings and underwear down. I peel them all the way down her legs, then toss them at that stupid wardrobe where they hit the wood, then fall to the floor with a muffled thump.

Outside the hotel window, raindrops pound against the street.

"Your mouth tastes sweet." I slide both hands under her ass cheeks. Squeeze and knead her, then lift her up for my inspection. "Like the toffees from the train. Are you sweet down here too?"

"Probably not," Madison says, so nervous, so breathless.

"Um, Ilya—"

I lick a stripe up the length of her seam.

Salty. Sweet. Tangy.

"Delicious," I tell her, and my sweet girl melts against the mattress again, relieved. She props herself up on her elbows and watches me, so greedy, as I seal my mouth between her legs and give her a different kind of kiss.

"Watch me," I rumble against her slick folds. Madison nods, not even blinking, and rests her legs on my shoulders. I kiss her thoroughly, *desperately*, like I could claim her this way. Like if I make this good enough for her, maybe she'll truly keep me.

I suckle every part of her. Slide my tongue past her entrance, delving deep. Rub my nose against her clit, my fingertips digging into her ass, then withdraw my aching tongue and lap at that tight bud.

Madison comes apart even harder than the train. Her whole body goes taut, her heels digging into my back, and she arches off the mattress like a bow string, moaning, guttural and perfect.

Slender fingers sink into my hair, tugging at the strands, and I could happily die down here, suffocating in her pleasure.

She sinks down with a happy sigh. Stops pulling my hair, and scratches idly at my scalp. Once she's caught her breath, her eyes flick down my body.

"Should I...?"

"No." I shove off the bed, striding to the window, chin slick. "There is no need."

"Oh. Okay." Madison almost sounds disappointed, but I don't turn around to check. I can't look at her. I can't let her see me like this—flayed open and wanting her so badly, for the first time I've known her, I feel truly insane.

Every part the dangerous man she once thought I was.

"Thank you, Ilya." She's so tentative, and *fuck*. I'm getting this all wrong.

I flick the edge of the curtain, staring down at the empty street. "You're very welcome, sweet girl."

There's a relieved sigh behind me, and then the creak of bed springs. When I risk a glance, Madison's curled on her side, facing away.

Good. Fine. It's better this way. I need to focus if I'm going to keep her safe.

If I'm going to spirit us both across an ocean, and help us start new lives together, safe from the bratva and her controlling father.

Madison

The harbor is quiet. Hushed in the pre-dawn gloom, the steel gray waves lapping at the stone walls while boats bob and clink. Overhead, seabirds wheel in flashes of white, and the ship, *our* ship, looms in the distance.

It moored twenty minutes ago. Ilya left me here, tucked away between stacks of lobster crates while he strode away toward the jetty, his broad shoulders thrown back, promising to come and fetch me if it's safe.

For a horrible stretch of minutes, I think maybe he's left me. Called his brother with my location, then disappeared on his own, our plan be damned. But then I remember the look on Ilya's face when we watched the news last night on our battered hotel TV—the announcement from my father that, after five days missing, he still refuses to bargain with the bratva. It doesn't matter *what* they threaten to do to me.

Dad put a real spin on it. Seriously, his PR guy must be hopping with glee. Such a *patriot*, a man who'd sacrifice his beloved daughter.

'Beloved' my ass. Watching his solemn face on the screen, I could have thrown a boot at him. I could have *screamed.* And when I glanced at Ilya, my cheeks flushed and my hands clammy, I saw my own rage reflected back at me.

My Russian was *pissed.* He freaking hates my dad more than I do. So I'm glad I'm taking a new name, letting my old life die here with the bratva.

"It's clear." Ilya's deep voice makes me jump. I spin around and find him at my elbow–apparently he snuck up behind me. The salty breeze tugs at his dark hair, and his slate gray eyes are probing, scanning me for any signs of distress under my jeans and winter coat.

He might look, but he doesn't touch. He hasn't for *days,* and I'm going crazy over here, every nerve in my body tingling whenever Ilya comes near.

"You know, you'd be a way better kidnapper than your brother. Even though you're twice his size, you're way more sneaky."

Ilya rolls his eyes, expression sour. "Thank you."

As we hurry toward the ship, we look like any other locals in this tired, lonely town–both dressed in faded, baggy winter clothes from the thrift store, with my hair tucked under a flat cap again. You wouldn't know, looking at us, that Ilya has diamonds in his duffel bag. That we're the ones everyone's searching for.

The new passport Ilya gave me is stiff in my pocket.

This is it. Our new chance.

My body lurches when I step on the ramp, the waves sending me staggering to the side. A big hand catches my elbow, and then Ilya's marching me onto the ship.

Cool, dark corridors, barely lit by cloudy portholes. Metal

walls and ceilings and floors, echoing with every step. We bought passage on the cheapest ship we could find, trying to avoid attention, and lord, it shows. I hope this rust bucket can make it across an entire ocean.

"It's better on the guest floors." Ilya's breath tickles my ear, and I scrabble blindly at his wrist until his hand wraps around mine, warm and steady. Metal creaks beneath our steps. "This is the working level. For the crew."

It *is* better on our floor, but only just. There are faded blue carpets and dull electric lights, and the portholes have been buffed clean to let in the sunrise.

We squeeze into our tiny cabin just as the sun bursts over the horizon, a ball of fire glinting off the choppy waves.

"Oh," I breathe, tugging at his hand. "*Ilya.*"

Lips graze against my temple. "Yes. I see it, beautiful girl."

It's the first time he's kissed me since… that night. The first time he's done anything more than hold my hand. And it's pathetic of me, but that brush of lips makes my body *sing;* it sends sparks cascading over my limbs.

I suck in a shaky breath, and when I turn to him, I can't stop staring at his gorgeous, craggy face. I can't believe this is happening. That he's running away with me.

Has anyone else in my whole life ever *chosen* me like this? Ever sacrificed for me?

No. I don't think so.

"Bunk beds." Ilya nods at the narrow mattresses, stacked against one wall. "You can take the top."

"If you like." I shrug, biting my lip. "I'd rather sleep down there. With you."

Gray eyes flutter shut, and he draws in a deep breath. His lips move, like he's counting to ten, like he's hanging by a thread.

And I *know* that he liked what we did–he's only holding back now out of some belated sense of honor.

I hide a grin.

This journey takes weeks, and this cabin is tiny. I'll be curled up on Ilya's chest within a day.

"Madison. Listen–"

The buzz of his phone cuts through the quiet. We both stare at his coat pocket, wearing matching frowns.

No one's called Ilya since we ran. Not even Vasily, not since that little *cut off her finger* chat.

"Um." I fiddle with my sleeve. God, I feel like a needy girlfriend. What is wrong with me? "Do you need to get that?"

Ilya digs out his phone and scowls at it, then turns it to face me, still ringing, his brother's name bright on the screen.

"Don't answer." Crap, I sound so desperate. Like if Ilya picks up that phone, he'll be choosing...

Well. Not me.

"I have to." His big thumb hovers over the button, and he doesn't look happy about it. My stomach clenches with dread. "Vasily might know something. We might not be safe, and an idiot like him will let it slip. *Da?*"

Ilya turns away, frowning out at the waves as he answers. But even from here, I can hear the phone line crackle, and he shakes his head, then stomps out into the corridor with a sigh.

Should I go after him?

Try to listen in?

Or cut my losses now, and get the hell off this ship before I lose a finger–or worse?

I sink down onto the bottom bunk, my legs like jelly, and my breaths are loud as I stare at Ilya's duffel bag, mind racing.

God, I can't believe he answered that freaking phone. Will he give me up?

Think, Madison.

I don't know this town. Don't have any other contacts I can trust. The police are corrupt, and my own father's given me up for dead. If I walk off this ship without Ilya, I'd better have a really good plan...

My palm is damp as I lift the duffel, weighing the bag stuffed full of cash and clothes and diamonds. I've got my new passport; my new identity. Could I do this without Ilya? Could I leave him here like this?

The ghost of his mouth grazes my temple. *I see it, beautiful girl.*

The duffel bag clatters against the floor, and I choke back a moan. I made my choice. I threw my lot in with this man–I decided to trust my captor.

Now it's time to see if I was right. I turn to face the cabin doorway, mouth dry.

Ilya

꩜

The phone signal is clearer on deck. Vasily's voice comes through loud in my ear, snide and furious.

"You stole yourself a little pet, did you, brother? That catch was *mine*."

Catch. Like she's a creature, not a girl. Like he dredged Madison up in one of those lobster crates. Ugh.

"She's no one's." The wind whips at my hair, and I watch impatiently as the crew folds up the ship ramp. We're preparing to launch. Getting away. I half expect to see a young woman with a flat cap and a duffel bag leap over that gap.

Could I blame her? Not really. Madison has no reason to trust anyone, least of all me. And as my brother rants and raves in my ear, giving me nothing but the words of a madman, I wish I'd never answered. She hates me now, surely. She'll think this a betrayal.

"Fuck." I hear a thump on the other end of the line. Something that sounds horribly like a splash. Then Vasily's yelling again, lecturing me on brotherly love. But I'm not listening to his words, not anymore–I'm staring around the cluttered deck, a sick feeling in my gut.

"You're here."

Vasily cuts off at once. His breaths puff loud down the phone, and then he chuckles. "Yes. I'm here. Where are you, brother? Don't you want to say hello?" More faint noises float through the phone, and it's a twisted echo of what I'm already hearing. The slosh of waves; the creak of thick ropes. The rumbling engine, spluttering to life, and the shouts of nearby crew, spit back into my ear a heartbeat later.

I whirl around, bile rising in my throat.

Ten steps away, Vasily smiles at me, the wet deck lurching beneath him.

"What?" He hangs up. Cocks his head. And his features are bruised and swollen, mottled purple like he's a piece of butcher's meat. "You didn't think I'd track my own brother's phone? I'd have been here sooner, but–" he waves at his ruined face; the ginger way he's favoring his left side "—the bosses wanted a word first."

"You shouldn't have followed."

Vasily barks out a laugh. "I had to, didn't I? She's my–"

"Your ticket to the big time." He's nodding. God, I hate this man. And I don't want to kill my own fucking brother, but I will. If it's the only way to keep Madison safe, I will. I show him that, too–not by pulling a knife or a gun, or some other shit. I don't need weapons, and Vasily knows it. I simply tuck my phone away and let my arms hang loose.

That manic grin fades. "What's your plan?" he spits. "Take her to a new location and call the bosses yourself?"

"No." Behind Vasily's shoulder, a pale face under a flat

cap pokes up behind a stack of crates. Madison's here, she's *listening*, and already my pulse picks up faster. I can't let him turn around, but I raise my voice a little. Let her hear me too. "I'm going to take care of her."

Vasily snorts. "You? She's using you, idiot. Girls like that don't want big bastards like you."

Maybe. Maybe not. Doesn't change things, either way. She's still *mine*. Mine to protect.

I shrug. "I don't care." And maybe that's the comment that breaks my brother–that breaks the final thread of his frayed control. Because Vasily snarls like an animal, charging lopsidedly toward me across the deck, and there's a glint of metal, a feminine shout, the hot bloom of pain as I lift his battered body overhead–

As I heave my brother over the ship's rail, I hear every insult he's ever hissed at me. I feel every punch he's ever given; every kick and shout and snide remark. I relive every nightmare, every betrayal, every day spent in fear. I've been under this man's thumb for most of my life, and as I shove him up towards the clouds, pain searing through my arm, I'm suddenly lighter than I've ever been.

Gone.

I clutch my arm, staring dry-eyed over the rail at the water below. White foam froths where Vasily went under, and he hasn't come up yet. He probably won't—a dip in those icy waters can be a death sentence all on its own.

All around us, crew members shout to each other as our ship pulls out to sea, no one even glancing over as the echoes of my brother's scream fades away.

"That was quick." A small voice pipes up by my elbow, and Madison grips the rail as she leans over. I puff out a pained breath and grab her hood, just in case. "Will he come after us again?"

"No. Be careful, please."

"Oh." She leans further over, ignoring me completely and chewing her lip. I grip her hood tighter. Then: "I'm sorry, Ilya. About your brother."

I grunt, and push away the second rush of memories. All the times when Vasily was—well, if not *kind*, then at least not violently awful. The shared meals. The long nights of vodka and gambling and watching mindless movies.

"And I'm sorry about your father."

It's her time to grunt, and it's such an unladylike noise that I grin, my cheeks aching, and my throat is so fucking tight as hot tears well in my eyes.

Vasily.

She's right. It was so quick. Too quick to know if I could have done things differently. If we could have come to some kind of arrangement, sent my brother back on land, back to try his luck with the bosses...

But no. Vasily was like a dog with a bone, and he would never have let Madison go. Not after getting his teeth into her.

"It's done," I announce, and I don't know whether it's for her benefit or mine. "I'm glad you stayed, sweet girl. Glad you trusted me."

Her throat bobs as she swallows. "Me too."

* * *

For the second time since I met her, Madison tends to my wounds. This time, it's not torn up knuckles—it's a deep slash cut along the outside of my arm, courtesy of Vasily's knife. It's bleeding steadily, my clothes sticking to the wound, and I hiss as I strip off my upper layers, my skin prickling in the cold air.

Madison clatters through the doorway, waving an ancient first aid kit. The bag is faded red, the handle held on by a thread, and she's triumphant. "Found one! The sailor I asked looked at me like a crazy person. Hey, are they still called sailors if the ship has no sails?"

Madison doesn't wait for an answer, sinking to her knees before me where I hunker on the bed, and she winces as she sees the cut. "Huh. That's, um. Ilya, a gash like that is a little above my pay grade."

"Just do your best." I don't tell her that to me, it's a paper cut. I've had plenty worse over the years, a few even from Vasily. "Cleaning it is the main thing."

"Sure. Okay. I can–I can do that." She rummages through the first aid kit, her icy blonde hair swinging forward. I can't help it: I lean forward and take a sniff. Madison smirks at me knowingly, but she doesn't stop hunting for supplies.

"Oh, here we go." The sting of antiseptic makes my teeth clench. "I can't believe you *lifted* him like that. You looked like–like one of those wrestlers, or something."

Yes, and I can't believe she *saw* it. I never wanted Madison to see me that way; to think of me as a violent brute, just like my brother said. I figured she'd run screaming in the other direction, and she'd be right.

But she doesn't *seem* scared of me, and if anything, her eyes are hungry as they track over my bare body. My thick arms, my chest hair, even the curve of my belly.

"Hey. Eyes on the prize." I lift my wounded arm, and Madison flushes, dabbing at the cut again with a stinging cloth.

"Shut up."

I grin, feeling light all of a sudden. Happier than I have in—well, years. The ship's engine rumbles underneath us, cleaving a path through those frozen waves, and we're really leaving. We really got away.

"What's your biggest wish for when we get there? For your new life?" I can't believe I haven't asked her this yet. It's like I haven't studied for the most important test of all.

Madison's plump mouth twists, and she frowns at my arm as she winds a bandage around the muscle. "*Our* new life. You mean like a white picket fence, or something?"

I frown, confused. Americans like fences? "Uh. Yes? If you like those."

Madison hums, and I hide my wince as she ties the bandage tight. It's good. It *should* be tight, and I won't make her feel bad about it. "I guess I... huh." Her shoulders slump. "I guess I've been told what to do by everybody for so long, I don't even know what I want. Isn't that pathetic?"

"No." I fix her with my sternest look. "You escaped from the bratva. You could never be pathetic."

"But if I have no idea what I want, how can I get it?"

I catch her hands in my own, cupping them between my palms. "You will figure it out. And good luck to any fool who then stands in your way."

Madison's nodding, looking thoughtful, still kneeling between my legs, and if I was a smart man, I'd sense the trap before she springs it. But I'm an old fool, and when she fixes me with a determined stare, I'm lost to her. A rabbit in a snare.

"I know one thing I want, Ilya. Definitely."

I nod. "Name it and it's yours."

Her palms settle on my thighs. "You."

117

Madison

My one-time captor reels back, his handsome face already shuttering. And I knew he'd be like this, the big jerk, even though he burned down his whole life for me, and we had that thing on the train, plus that one perfect night in the hotel that changed *everything*.

"Ilya," I warn, gripping harder at his thighs. "Don't you dare. Don't protect me from this. From you."

"Well *someone* should."

"No." I elbow his knees wider, then shuffle closer on the cabin floor, so close his legs brush the sides of my waist. His heat of his bare chest washes over my front, and I can taste his masculine scent in the air; I can smell the coppery tang of his blood seeping through that bandage.

Ilya watches me, his eyes tight and his jaw clenched, and he looks more exhausted than I've ever seen him. He looks...

Miserable.

Ouch. The deep breath I take–it *hurts*, but even though it's like prodding a bruise, I still need him to say it. I need to be sure. "You don't want me, then?"

It's okay if he doesn't. I mean, it'll be a punch to the gut, but I'll respect it. I'll find a way to be around this gruff, perfect man without mooning all over him, my longing written all over my face.

It'll take a while, though. Because even though I've only known Ilya less than a week, he already feels... essential. Like drinking water. Breathing air. But–

"Don't want you?" His laugh is bitter. Broken. "This is not the issue, sweet girl." His mouth twists, and then he's reaching up with trembling fingers. Tucking a lock of hair behind my ear. "I *imprisoned* you. I held you captive for my brother. It doesn't matter how badly I want you now, you understand?"

Oh, I understand. I understand this big idiot perfectly.

"Move, please." I prod at the muscled slabs of his chest, and Ilya leans back automatically, though he winces at his mistake when I climb onto his lap, straddling him on the lower bunk and gripping his broad shoulders. His skin is soft, burning hot under my palms, and I can't help squeezing. Marveling at how *built* he is.

Like he could stop a runaway train with an outstretched hand.

Which is lucky, because I'm wheeling out of control, thundering a hundred miles an hour down the rails myself.

"It was... a strange way of meeting." Ilya scoffs but I keep going, fixing him with a glare. I need him to know I mean this. "And I blamed you at first, I didn't trust you at all, but I know now that you were trapped too. Just trying to hold everything together; trying to find a way through for both of us. And you've *proven*–" I thump his uninjured arm "—so many freaking times that you wouldn't let anything bad happen to me. You were my captor, yes, but my protector too. You're the first person who's given me freedom, given me *choices* in my whole life."

My throat sticks as I swallow. My heart's pounding against my chest, and I ask the most important question of all. "I can forget all that bad stuff, Ilya. Can you?"

Those tired eyes flutter closed, and for a second, I can't breathe. My ears are ringing; the cabin's tilting; waves lap at the ship's sides. I told him all that, I spilled out my whole soul, and maybe it didn't work. It wasn't enough.

"Madison."

I sag on his lap, defeated. My hands slip off his shoulders and land on my thighs. I need to climb off him, but my limbs won't cooperate.

"*Madison.*"

"I'm-I'm going."

Ilya frowns, eyes still closed, and then two big hands grip my waist, pinning me in place. "*No.*"

...No?

That's it?

I bare my whole heart to this ass, and all I get in return is 'no'? I scowl, lips parting, and I'm ready to curse him out better than any sailor on board.

"You don't get to boss me around, Ilya, not anymore–"

The hands on my waist jerk me forward, and then I'm plastered to his warm chest, and he's *kissing* me. His lips move against mine, and he angles his head, probing deeper, and holy shit, it's like he's finally communicating with me. Telling me without words exactly how badly he wants me.

And judging by this kiss... by his bruising grip on my waist, by the hot slide of his tongue and the growl rumbling in his chest...

He wants me really freaking badly.

"Ilya," I gasp, head spinning. My Russian grunts and kisses me harder. When he finally tears his head away, his lips are damp and his eyes are wild. Ilya squeezes me impossibly tighter, but weirdly, I don't care.

I *like* him gripping me like this—desperately. Possessively. Like he can't stand even a few air molecules to come between his hands and my body.

"Please," I say, and finally, *finally,* he nods.

Then Ilya reaches between us, grips two handfuls of my jeans, and tears a gaping hole at the seams.

* * *

I stare, wordless. Can't even comprehend. Then my brain comes back online, and I tip my head back and howl with laughter, the sound bouncing around our metal cabin.

My jeans-ripper watches with a rueful smile. "You want the real Ilya, yes?" His thumbs trace the frayed edges of the tear, dipping closer and closer to the fabric of my panties. "The real Ilya is a bad man. He tears up jeans to get at your pussy."

Holy hell, I shouldn't be so into this. Shouldn't be so freaking turned on by that animal display. But hey, I didn't even like these jeans, not really, and I'll celebrate their noble sacrifice to the cause.

Because Ilya's thumbs have found my heat. The damp, aching heat of my *pussy*, as he calls it, scorching through the scrap of lace between my thighs. And these really are my favorite panties, damn me, but I still gasp out, "Rip them off too, Ilya. Please."

121

He does it easily. With barely a flex of muscle. And then I'm squirming on his lap, cool air washing over my sex, and I need him so badly I can't think straight. My fingers tremble where they cup the sides of his neck; my breaths shudder in and out of my lungs.

"Please, Ilya." My hips rock uselessly against the empty air. "I want you to take me. Please."

He grunts again, and I'll never get sick of that sound. His gruff, deep, male satisfaction, as he tugs his own jeans open and pulls his thick, ruddy shaft out between us.

It's… big. Bigger than I expected, somehow, even though I've freaking met Ilya before and, well, it's all in proportion. But my mouth goes dry, and even as the hunger crackles through my body, as I look at him, I can't help the sinking feeling.

"You will do it," Ilya says quietly, like he's read my mind. "You will take it, Madison. You will take my cock like the brave girl you are."

And it's not an order, coming from him. It's support. A vote of confidence. He believes in me so strongly, insists that I'm a fighter, someone to admire, and I grit my teeth, so determined as I wrap my hand around him.

That newborn confidence falters almost immediately. Holy shit, my fingers and thumb don't meet. He's *thick* as well as long, and does he seriously think I can take this inside me?

"Brave girl," Ilya murmurs, and then I'm nodding again. Shuffling forward and notching his broad head at my entrance.

Resistance. My body fights him at first. It's alien, an intrusion, something I've never welcomed inside me before—but Ilya's fingertips graze along my jaw, and I gust out a breath. Feel some of the tension seep from my frame.

"Slowly." One hand grips my hip, stilling me. The other slips between us, thick fingers rubbing at my clit, and though he's barely got an inch inside, my hips jerk. I tip my head back with a moan. "We will do this properly. With patience and no pain. We'll make you slick and ready for me, until you're *begging* me to fuck you deeper."

It seems so unlikely, so impossible, but with every sweep of Ilya's fingers over my clit, the tingle between my legs grows stronger. Without thinking, I'm rolling my hips. Urging him further and further inside me.

"Good girl." His approval sends heat flooding through my veins. I gasp, sinking down another inch. "You see? So perfect. So brave."

All this time, Ilya's sitting beneath me on the bottom bunk, so sturdy and patient. Not moving an inch, besides the delicious swirl of his fingertips on my clit. And I want more, I want to see him affected by this too, so I lean forward, and as I take him deeper, I suck a kiss against his neck.

It's sloppy. Hungry. Untutored and wild, and maybe I'd be embarrassed if Ilya didn't groan from the depths of his stomach. Beneath me, his hips thrust, that thick shaft moving inside me, and though he stutters out an apology and settles down against the bed, that's what I *want*.

Both of us. Doing this together.

"Fuck me." It's like someone else's voice. Someone else's words. The old Madison would never do this, not any of it, and she'd certainly never beg a mobster to bounce her on his cock in a cramped ship's cabin. But that old Madison was a shadow, a pale imitation of how I feel in this moment, and when Ilya curses and swallows, I chase the bob of his throat with my tongue. "Fuck me, Ilya. Do it. *Please.*"

My Russian curses loudly, fluidly, then grips both my hips

and slams up inside me.

Yes.

He's nearly there. Nearly all the way in, so unbelievably hard and thick, throbbing as he drags in and out of my pussy. One more slam, and another, brutal enough to make my teeth click, and–

"Madison." Ilya's damp forehead presses against mine. His eyes are screwed shut tight, like he's in pain. "Madison. My sweet girl."

Then he opens his eyes, pinning me with that slate gray gaze, and I'm lost to him. Shoving my knees wider so I can take him deeper, hips rolling, cheeks flushed. *He* may be worried, guilt etched on that handsome face, but I'm having the time of my freaking life. And Ilya finally seems to get that, thank god, because he lets out another one of those toe-curling growls, and then we're moving again.

Together.

Brutal.

Perfect.

"Mine," Ilya grunts between thrusts, as if I'd ever argue that. Hell yeah, I'm his. And he's *mine.*

"My mobster," I grit out between panted breaths, and he nods, stern and final. This is it. This is us.

When Ilya slides a hand between us, rubbing at my clit again, it's like striking a match. I'm burning up, caught in a blast of heat, and as I clamp down on him, I can feel every ridge and vein of him, pulsing inside me. I moan and shiver and tremble and shake, and when I finally collapse back onto Ilya's lap, I'm like a puppet with cut strings. I couldn't help any more if I tried.

But Ilya smirks, taking my waist in that punishing grip, and with three more snaps of his hips, he stiffens too. Floods me with sticky warmth—so much it drips onto his thighs.

It takes nearly a minute to catch my breath.

Then I stare around, dismayed, and say, "We really did a number on this cabin."

Ilya peers around too at the rumpled bed sheets, already stained; the scattered, torn clothes and the kicked over first aid kit, band aids strewn over the floor. The smell of sex is heavy in the air, and we're both so flushed that Ilya's bare chest is practically steaming in the cold.

Ilya shrugs. I press my lips together against the giggles. "We also threw a man off their deck," he points out.

I snort. "Worst passengers ever."

Oh well. I hope the neighbors don't hate us too badly, because it's a long journey ahead of us across the ocean.

The journey home. To our new lives—together.

I wrap my arms around Ilya's neck. I may never let go.

Ilya

~ ✦ ~

*F*ive years later

The sound of squealing leads me through our kitchen and out into the grassy backyard. It's a hazy evening, the sky tinged pink as clouds drift over the rooftops, and the scent of nearby bonfires fills the air.

I didn't understand Madison's comment about white picket fences, back when I first asked what she wanted from life. And I think she was joking back then, poking fun at the idea, but now that we have a home together and our daughters are playing in the yard...

It doesn't seem like a funny thing to want. Not at all.

Not after growing up with Vasily and the bratva, scraping by and bleeding for our existence. Not after so many years of pain and loneliness and fear.

No—our simple, bright house with its emerald green lawn is... paradise.

"Good day at work?"

Madison knows I'm behind her before I say anything. I wrap my arms around her waist and sink my chin onto her shoulder, grunting in reply. There were a lot of meetings today, and that always makes me grumpy, but they were satisfying, at least. Lucrative. And I don't mind putting those old cutthroat business skills from the bratva to use again when they buy *this*. A safe, happy home for Madison and our daughters.

"Did you paint?" She nods, and I glance at the artist's cabin we built her last summer in the corner of the yard. I'll go and look later, when I have time to linger. Appreciate her skill.

"It's not bad, is it?" Madison whispers, and I know what she means. She's talking about *this*–the sunset, the children's laughter, the fresh start we built for ourselves. It wasn't so long ago that we stepped off that ship with a duffel bag stuffed with diamonds.

We still have them, tucked safely away in a bank vault. I suppose we're both cautious, after everything. Needing to have a back up plan.

"It's perfect." My words sound gruff, coming out too hard, but my wife understands me. She tips her head back and melts against my shoulder with a sigh. "Come upstairs." I nip her earlobe, and a shiver rolls through her soft body. "The babysitter just arrived. She's dropping her bag in the kitchen."

Madison snorts. "We're supposed to go *out*. Not lock ourselves away in the bedroom like... like..."

"Like desperate lovers?"

Another strangled laugh. "Yeah. Like that."

"A hotel, then." I twirl the curling ends of her hair. "If you're feeling prudish, sweet girl."

I deserve the elbow jabbing into my gut. But I'm grinning when she turns, and Madison's smirking at me too, and she leans against my chest. Tips her face up and whispers, warm and breathless, "Yes. A hotel."

Fuck. How did a mobster ever get so lucky? I can't make sense of it, especially when slender fingers spread over my shirt and she adds, "Tie me up, will you? For old times' sake."

Old times' sake. Ha. If 'old times' were last week.

"You won't escape me." Her wrist is delicate in my grip, and I tug her over to our daughters so we can both wish them goodnight.

Perhaps I'll gag her, too. But not for too long—I like to hear my wife's moans. I like to hear her beg.

That babysitter can't come out here fast enough.

My wife and I have memories to make.

III

Big Beast

Description

H e's the city's top chef. **Famously strict, with a trademark scowl.**

I'm the waitress who just ruined his night.

Look, I'm not always this clumsy. I *never* drop plates at work. But for the last two days, the walls have been spinning around me; the floors have dipped and lurched under my feet.

Vertigo, the doctor says. *It will go away soon.* But in the meantime, a girl's gotta eat. I need this job–and I figure, how wrong can one shift go?

So wrong. So horribly wrong.

And now Chef Fontaine *hates* me. He looks at me like I'm dirt on his shoe, and he fires me so loudly, every worker in the whole restaurant hears.

I think I've hit rock bottom. There's no lower I can go.

Then Chef Fontaine turns up at my apartment, that scowl fixed on his face, and I realize… the gorgeous jerk's not through with me yet.

Matthieu

I stare at the crowd gathered around me, and I do *not* look at the sweet, curvy waitress huddled near the back. No matter how badly I want to look at her, no matter how I want to soak up the sight of her–I keep my gaze elsewhere.

It's twenty minutes until we open for the night, and every surface of the kitchen gleams. There's no time for my unhealthy obsession with that young woman. The kitchen staff are all dressed in matching snowy white, while the servers are in crisp, flawless black, and they're all waiting for me. Waiting for my words.

She looks delicious in her server's tunic. Her warm brown skin looks butter-soft, and tendrils of her glossy dark hair have escaped, curling around her temples.

Chloe Fray. Her name has been etched on my brain since the first day I heard it, though I've never said it out loud. There's no reason for the Head Chef to take such an interest in a server. But Chloe shifts awkwardly at the back of the crowd, her eyes darting around the kitchen, and briefly, I wonder what's bothering her.

Focus, you fool.

I drag my gaze away from her, annoyed at myself. This is it. Tonight is the night. The biggest critic in the city is coming to my restaurant.

"Are all the ingredients prepped?"

My sous chef answers, his confident voice ringing through the room. "Yes, Chef."

"And the restaurant? Are the tables ready?"

The head server pipes up: "Yes, Chef Fontaine."

The workers shift nervously as I stare around them, letting my gaze rove slowly through the crowd. I know the nickname they call me when they think I'm not listening. *The Beast.* Perhaps it's a reference to my unusual size–my barrel chest and solid belly. My thick arms and long legs.

Or perhaps I've earned that name in other ways. After all, I am a very demanding man. I accept nothing less than perfection.

But you don't become one of the top chefs in the city by letting standards slide.

"I don't need to tell you who will be here tonight." The critic is a renowned man in his own right, as famous as any of the restaurants he reviews. He's exacting; very difficult to please. A positive review from a man like that will be worth ten reviews from kinder critics. "I expect a flawless performance from all of you."

"Yes, Chef," the crowd mumbles together.

My eyes are drawn back to her. The nervous waitress. *Chloe.* The beautiful girl I've spent weeks–no, *months*–pretending I don't notice, ever since her first shift in my kitchen.

She looks different tonight. A little twitchy. Ashen, even. Is she up to this?

I push the thought away, picking an imaginary speck of lint off my sleeve. *Focus, Matthieu.*

If my staff aren't feeling well, they don't come in. That's what the generous sick pay I provide is for. Most likely, she's picked up on the nerves in the room–the sense that if I make it, we *all* make it. We all go higher, with wages rising and tips coming from wealthier diners.

It's a lot of pressure running a restaurant like this. Every person here, from the newest pot wash to my second in command, burns with ambition. They wouldn't work for the Beast otherwise.

I end the huddle quickly. There's no need to linger, not with so much to be done, and unlike other chefs, I've no love for the sound of my own voice. I'd rather be cooking, *creating*, finding that blissful, dreamlike state that I'm always reaching for in my work.

The critic is coming tonight, but I am not too concerned. The kitchen is spotless, my staff are disciplined, and I hand-pick every ingredient that enters this building.

So I've got a good feeling. The lights are bright; the scents of the kitchen are crisp. My favorite beautiful server is here, nervous or no, and although I'd sound crazy if I admitted it out loud, I've often thought of Chloe as my good luck charm.

I allow myself one final glimpse of her before I turn away. She stands with hands grasped behind her back, her tunic hugging those generous curves, watching me with big, brown eyes. Temptation incarnate. Her lips are pressed in a firm line, but when she sees me looking, she gives a tiny smile.

God. It's nothing more than a twitch of her full lips, but my body heats in response. My muscles tense; my skin prickles.

My heart races beneath my chef's jacket.

I turn and stride across the kitchen, my steps light.

Tonight I'm going to cook something wonderful. I know it.

* * *

It's *parfait*. Better than I've ever cooked before–and please excuse my ego, but that is saying something. One hour in, and I already know this evening is blessed. There is a special alchemy happening in my kitchen.

Knives glint. Flames lick at saucepans. The room is filled with mouthwatering scents and the organized chaos of a kitchen working at full tilt. We're working together, no, *dancing* together, to the beat of wooden spoons and the hiss of steam, but there's more than that. We're cooking something magical tonight.

That one tiny smile from Chloe–it lit me up from the inside. Spurred me on to new creative heights. That critic won't know what hit him, and perhaps it's overeager of me, but I'm already smug, thinking of his glowing review in tomorrow's paper.

Perhaps I should speak to Chloe one day soon after all. If this is what a single one of her smiles can do to me, imagine her *words*. Imagine what I might create if I ever heard her laugh, or if she'd only let me tuck one of those stray curls behind her delicate ear. I'm her boss, yes, and judging by my nickname, I am a difficult man to know. But that *smile*...

She wouldn't smile like that at a man she hated. Would she?

"Watch it," Pablo says at my elbow, and I jerk back to life, rescuing the sea bass sizzling in its pan. A few more seconds, and it would have burned–and once that acrid scent enters a kitchen, it permeates *all* the food. I nod at my sous chef,

136

grateful but unsettled. A minute's distraction, and I nearly ruined everything. So much for a blessed kitchen.

"Nerves are normal. Human, even."

I scoff, my forehead etched with a scowl as I spoon lemon-scented broth into the pan. "Nerves are for lesser chefs, Mendoza."

It's an asshole thing to say, but Pablo doesn't call me out on it. Most likely, he can read the strain on my brow. He'll mock me for such nonsense on another night, a safer night, one when all of our careers aren't dangling on a thread, and when he does, I'll laugh and let him.

Hell, I'll even buy him a drink to smooth over my harsh words. Unlike most of my staff, my second in command is not afraid of me. He's seen me at my lowest, and he has more faith in me than anyone here–except maybe myself.

Again, that tiny smile flickers across my brain.

"Pass the garlic." Pablo obeys immediately, his movements smooth and efficient. Too late, I remember to grumble: "Thank you."

His snort makes me wince, but we keep working. Chopping and stirring. And there's a comfort to it, a rhythm we find together that goes deeper than any verbal conversation. We're fine. Pablo is not offended, and I haven't blundered this night just yet. I haven't wasted the gift of Chloe's smile.

This is for her, I decide as I plate up the critic's entree. It's flawless: a work of mouthwatering beauty, perfectly arranged on a warm, white plate. Tender fish and crisp, vibrant vegetables. A sauce drizzled in an artful swoop. Pride pulses in my chest, and I'm fiercely satisfied as I ring the bell for a server.

I hope Chloe catches a glimpse of this plate. We may not

have spoken, I may only be her boss, but these days, everything I cook is a tribute to her.

Chloe

ertigo. *Vertigo.* When the doctor gave his verdict yesterday, I couldn't believe it, never mind that the room was spinning.

I'm a waitress. A waitress with *bills*, and rent coming due, and now an elderly neighbor who can't afford her weekly groceries. I can't afford to lose my balance like this, the floor pitching and rolling under every step I take, and I *definitely* can't afford to miss a shift and lose the customers' tips.

Those tips keep me afloat. They keep the landlord from knocking on my door. Missing a Friday night shift? It's not an option.

That's what I thought, anyway, when I forced myself out of bed earlier. The room spun so horribly when I was in the shower, I braced my hands on my knees and retched until my chest ached. My head was pounding worse than a drum, and my skin was too hot, too tingly, but I figured it would ease off.

I was determined to make it work, and until I arrived at Chez Fontaine for my shift, I had no idea tonight was such a big deal.

The critic is here. *The* critic.

And I've already smashed two plates, damn it.

I didn't mean to, obviously. I'm *never* clumsy normally–I take pride in being able to balance several loaded plates on my arms, weaving between tables like a circus performer. And I wasn't serving *him*, thank goodness. One plate, I dropped in the safety of the kitchen, and the other on the outskirts of the room, cringing at the sound of shattering china as heads turned my way.

Chef Fontaine hasn't noticed yet, too wrapped up in tonight's menu. But once he does, I'm totally screwed. The Beast doesn't allow room for error–he is flawless in his own work, and we must be too. Only the best are allowed to work in Chez Fontaine.

Usually, I kind of love that about him. His *intensity*, his constant striving, his handsome scowl, the way a lock of his brown hair hangs over his brow when he stands over the oven, an artist creating his great works. Sometimes, on quiet shifts, I find excuses to linger in the kitchen just so I can watch him. Just so I can be *near* him, my heart racing under my pressed black tunic.

Sometimes... I think he feels me nearby too. His head twitches to the side, like he's searching for me. Like he's watching me back out of the corner of his eye.

But that's crazy. And no amount of crazy wishful thinking will excuse those smashed plates once he hears what I've done.

"Chloe." The head server–a middle aged woman with a severe blonde bun–beckons me into the kitchen as I carry a stack of dirty plates back inside. My stomach roils as I walk, sweat beading my upper lip, and I'm gripping these plates so tight, my knuckles turn pale.

The walls spin and tilt.

The floor shifts beneath my feet.

Oh *lord,* I should not have come here tonight. I need to go home. I need to lie down for about a week. But once I do, they'll be short staffed, and my neighbor Mrs Spinelli needs food for the month, and those *tips*–

I push all the clamoring thoughts away. There's only room for one thought in my aching brain right now, and that is: *get through this, Chloe.* I make it to the dish washing station on wobbly legs, feeling as relieved as a shipwreck survivor reaching land, then unload my plates to a harried pot wash.

Gripping the counter, I turn to the head server, ears ringing. "Yes?"

"Order up." The head server gives me an odd look, her gaze dropping down my body and back up, but I force myself to stand straight. I paste a placid smile onto my face, never mind the queasy twisting of my stomach, and follow her nod toward the plating station.

I can do this. I can deliver a plate without courting disaster. Even when I find Chef Fontaine lingering at the station fussing over the entree, all big, burly shoulders and graying temples, I swallow hard and tell myself to keep going.

"Wish me luck." The Beast glances up, eyes warming as he watches me approach, those words so deep and delicious with the hint of his French accent. And he–he *winks* at me, such a quick, subtle movement that I almost think I dreamed it. The Beast, winking at his server with those dreamy hazel eyes? Impossible. The man is made of stone.

But he's still watching me, something like heat in his gaze, and… oh, hell. On a normal day, I'd flush to the roots of my hair under that stare. But tonight, with the room spinning and my heart racing in the very worst way, it's all I can do to reach out and pick up the plate.

"Good luck," I whisper, wincing as the plate tilts in my clumsy grip and a vegetable shifts, smearing a path through the drizzled sauce. Chef Fontaine twitches, staring hard at his ruined presentation, and a thick silence stretches between us.

The Beast says nothing. Not a word. I don't know whether I want to laugh or cry about that.

So I do neither, and instead I clear my throat, then turn on my heel and lurch toward the dining area, bright spots floating before my eyes. And with every step, his food is jolted worse. The presentation ruined a little more. I stare down at the plate in my hands, tears brimming in my eyes, and I've never felt so freaking ashamed.

I shouldn't have come tonight. Shouldn't have picked up this plate, because I've ruined it. All his hard work—all *everyone's* hard work, undone in a few seconds by me.

Oh god. I swallow hard, tongue thick.

I'm so fired after this.

* * *

I've never lost a job before. That thought chases through my dizzy brain, round and round as Chef Fontaine glares at me in the center of the kitchen. We're squaring off, his strong, tall body towering over my short, plump one, and I can barely keep my eyes open without wanting to retch.

Never lost a job before.

I've always been a good worker, cheerful and reliable. I've never missed a shift or had a complaint against my name. And

I guess I always figured if I *did* get fired it wouldn't be like this—like a public execution.

I didn't think I'd be standing in the center of a busy kitchen, my tunic stained with food I could never afford to eat myself. Not with the crash of breaking china ringing in my brain, along with the gasps of the diners as they all turned to stare.

Not with a crowd of wide-eyed spectators, wincing on my behalf as Chef Fontaine tears me down to the floor with his words.

I didn't think *this* man would be the one to do it. After all, ever since I first laid eyes on him, I've always known I'd rather chop off a limb than disappoint him.

"Sabotage," the Beast growls, the word tossed between us like a grenade. "Is that it? One of my competitors paid you to do this? To ruin my career in one fucking swoop?"

In one fucking swoop. That phrase is oddly delicious in his accent.

Huh. I think I might be delirious.

"No, Chef." I answer him a beat too late, my words weirdly muffled in my own head, like they're coming from far, far away. I squeeze the hem of my stained tunic, heart lurching, palms damp. "I'm so sorry." And I am. I'm so freaking sorry.

If I could wind back the clock, I'd stay safely in bed. I'd call in sick, never mind the bills and the groceries. I'd figure out another way. Because—

"In his *lap.*" Chef Fontaine stares at me like he's never seen me before. That flash of heat and playfulness from earlier is long gone, and in its place is only ice and rage. "You tossed the critic's food into his fucking lap. And you expect me to believe this was a mistake?"

My nod makes the room tilt wildly. I slam my eyes shut,

swallowing hard.

"Yes," I whisper. "Or–no. I don't expect you to believe that. But it's–"

"The truth?" Chef Fontaine's voice is harsh. Everyone in the kitchen is holding their breath, the tension thick in the air, and when he laughs, I'm not the only one who cringes. I hear the rustle of fabric, the uncomfortable murmurs. Can practically taste their relief that this is happening to me, not them.

He's called the Beast for a reason. He's always been strict, with a short fuse. But he's always been fair, too, and never once have I seen him humiliate someone publicly like this.

Lucky me.

"Perhaps you could continue this in your office, Chef."

I squint one eye open and offer a grateful smile to the sous chef, Pablo Mendoza. He's a few years younger than Chef Fontaine, and he doesn't have the same gravity, but he's the bravest soul here. The only person willing to stand up to the boss in a moment like this.

We both know it's no use, but it's kind of him to try and spare me this nightmare. But the sight of me smiling at Pablo seems to push Chef Fontaine over a precipice, and when I look at him again, visceral hatred burns in his eyes. His anger's so hot, I half expect sparks to rain down on the tiles.

"No need," the Beast spits. My stomach sinks. I know it's coming, but every word still lands like a blow.

I've admired this man for so long; I've *longed* for him, in the quiet hours of the night. My crush is private, but no less potent for that fact. But Chef Fontaine's voice is cold and empty when he says my name for the first time: "You are done here, Chloe. Get out."

Ouch.

No need to tell me twice. I don't even blame him, and that's the worst part. I let Chef Fontaine down; let *everyone* here down. I deserve everything he's said and more.

I turn around, room tilting, eyes burning, and stagger for the door.

Matthieu

I have fired plenty of employees over the years. My standards are high, and while I don't try to make a habit of it, I'm also not afraid to let the bad workers go. Firing staff is a fact of life for the owner and Head Chef of a restaurant, and it has never once bothered me before.

I've never had second thoughts. Never felt a twinge of guilt. And I've *definitely* never felt a strange longing for the person I let go. But Chloe Fray was... different. Special to me, in some private, shameful way.

Less than twenty four hours later, I miss her. Thoughts of her kept me up for hours last night, tossing and turning, and every time I close my eyes, I see her pretty round face.

Now, I keep glancing around the kitchen, automatically searching for a glimpse of her glossy dark hair, even though I fired her last night.

How ridiculous.

"Good afternoon." I stride out of my office, tone brisk. I've been here for hours, but the first, eager workers are arriving for the evening shift. Chloe would normally be among them. She was always on time, always impeccably dressed, always so *polite—*

It doesn't make any sense.

I push the thought away.

Pablo nods at me from where he's wiping down a counter, stainless steel surfaces glinting all around him. I nod back before calling out to the staff already here. "We're running an updated menu tonight. Servers, please memorize the new specials. Allergen information is on file."

It's nothing unusual, but they're shifty, glancing at each other out of the corners of their eyes. I raise an eyebrow at Pablo, and reluctance is etched on his face, but he jerks his chin at my office.

He won't bullshit me. I'm lucky I have Pablo. And less than a minute later, the door shuts behind us, muffling the clangs and mutters of the kitchen. I turn to my sous chef, and a headache already has my skull in a vice grip, squeezing my throbbing temples.

"Alright, what is it? The review's not out, so that can't be the issue. Not yet."

Pablo's mouth twists. "It's Chloe Fray."

At the sound of her name, my heart plummets, then bounces off the tiles and back into my chest. Hope—ridiculous, mis-placed hope—lifts my chin.

"Oh." I aim for casual. "Is she here?"

Pablo snorts, and that hope sours as quickly as it came. "No, she's not here. You think she'd come back after last night?"

I suppose not. It was an unmitigated disaster, and beyond that, I was rather harsh. My anger was sharp, *brutal,* slicing up my insides. But even if she forgot something and came to collect her belongings, that would be *something*. Another stolen glimpse.

God, there's something wrong with me. That young woman single-handedly botched my career in one evening, and here I am longing for a final snatched moment with her. Pathetic.

"Then what about Chloe Fray?" I don't have time for guessing games. That review may ruin me when it comes out, but until then, I have a restaurant to run. Food to prepare.

"Some of the staff are worried about her."

I scrub a hand down my face, already exhausted by this nonsense. Will they still feel *sorry* for her if that review forces them all out of jobs? If it emerges, as it surely will, that one of the rival restaurants paid her to ruin all our careers?

"They're annoyed because I fired her?"

Pablo frowns. "They're annoyed because she was clearly ill. The girl could barely see straight, and you tossed her onto the street at night."

No. No, no, no. That is *not* what happened. I would never–she wasn't–

"She was not *ill*. This restaurant has a generous sick pay policy."

Pablo's head tilts, and he almost looks sorry for me. "More generous than the tips the servers get?"

Fuck. What? No.

No, this isn't happening. That is *not* what happened last night. Even if I knew for a fact that Chloe took a bribe to ruin my restaurant–hell, even if she tossed food at the walls and ran naked past the diners–I would never toss her onto the street if I thought she was ill. I'd fire her, yes, but I'd escort her home safely myself.

The memory of her ashen face drifts through my mind,

unbidden.

It was dark last night. The city can be dangerous. Did she get home okay? Fuck.

"Her number." My voice is hoarse. "Get me Chloe's number. I'll call and make sure she's okay. But she wasn't ill, alright? She can't have been."

Because how could I live with that? It's impossible. I can't contemplate it.

"The staff like Chloe." Pablo's fingers fly over the keyboard, his slender body perched behind my desk. A frown pinches his eyebrows as he scans the computer screen. "If you assure them she's okay, they'll forget this. Move on."

"I will. I'll tell them." Once I know it's not a lie.

The phone rings for an eternity. I grip the handset tight, my jaw clenched as I stare blindly at the wall. Behind the desk, Pablo shifts awkwardly, his head tipped as he tries to listen in.

"It's ringing," I tell him pointlessly. Obviously it's ringing. I'm not calling my ex-employee to simply breathe down the phone.

Every second that stretches on makes my palms sweat. Every moment without hearing her voice, my heart sinks another inch.

Then: "Hello?"

It's her. Chloe. Though we never spoke directly until last night, I'd recognize her warm, husky voice any day. And hearing her now, I gust out a relieved breath, even as a voice whispers in my head that she sounds weak. Exhausted.

"Chloe. This is Matthie—Chef Fontaine."

"Oh." Chloe sucks in a shaky breath. "Um. Is there—is there a problem with my paperwork?"

Right. Because I fired this woman yesterday.

"No." I scrub a palm over my jaw, my stubble crackling. Is this the most awkward conversation of my whole life? Quite possibly. "Some of the staff are concerned that you were unwell last night."

There's a long pause. An agonizing pause.

Then it all pours out in a damning rush.

"Oh god, I'm so sorry, Chef Fontaine. I knew I was ill–the doctor said it's vertigo–but I couldn't afford to miss a shift, and I thought I could get through it okay. But that was so selfish of me and I can't believe I hurt your chances with that critic like that, because you worked so hard and I'm so ashamed–"

I hold the phone away from my ear, staring at the handset. The sound of her babbling drifts through the quiet office, but I barely hear it. My ears are ringing.

"She's ill?" Pablo's mouth turns down at the corners when I nod. He's not happy. Well, that makes two of us.

God, what have I done? I hang up without thinking, then curse under my breath. Just another thing to apologize for.

"I'm leaving." My fingers are clumsy as I tug at my chef's collar. It's too tight, suddenly. Suffocating. "You can handle the menu tonight, can't you?"

"Of course." Pablo watches, startled, as I snatch up my keys and wallet, shoving them in my pockets. "Where are you–"

"I'm going to check on Chloe Fray."

"Oh." He glances over my shoulder at the closed office door. "Should I tell them that?"

"If you like." Leaning past my sous chef to the computer screen, I tap Chloe's address into my phone. "I don't really care."

And I don't. They can like me or not. They can work for me or not. Their choices and their feelings won't keep me up at night. But *I* need to damn well live with myself, and last night I apparently tossed a sick woman out onto the street.

I need to find her. Chloe Fray is special, and in the darkest recesses of my brain… she's *mine*.

I need to make sure with my own two eyes that she is okay.

Chloe

I f I lie spread-eagled on my bed and keep very, very still... this is not so bad. I don't feel like I'm dying at all. Sure, the framed pictures on my walls seem to pulse and shift when I look at them, and the night robe hanging on my bedroom door looks like it's melting onto the floorboards. And yes, I'm still queasy with shame over what I did at the restaurant–especially after hearing Chef Fontaine's gravelly baritone asking whether I'm well.

Am I well? No. Because I still can't stand up without the whole room tilting to the side, and more than that, because I got *fired.*

I still can't believe it. My whole life, I've been such a good girl, and now I've been fired. And I deserved it, too! I spilled food all over the harshest critic in the city. Every single person in that restaurant must be cursing my name.

Mashing my face into the bed, I say a little prayer. Lord, please let this mattress suck me down and swallow me whole. I can never show my face outside this apartment again.

Thump. Thump. Thump.

Is that the door? Or my pulse pounding in my skull?

Thump. Thump. "Miss Fray?"

Shoot. I'd know that deep voice anywhere, tinged with a faint French accent. I hear that voice in my dreams; it growls phrases over and over in my head on a never-ending loop. Things like: *Servers to me, please* and *Desserts are ready!*

Because hey, before yesterday, Chef Fontaine had never spoken a word to me one-on-one. Though I guess after last night, I can add one more phrase: *You're done here, Chloe. Get out.*

Get out.

Get out.

"Miss Fray?"

Whimpering, I snatch a pillow and flatten it over my face. Soft cotton brushes against my feverish cheeks, and the stubby end of a feather pokes my forehead. Why is he here? Wasn't firing me once enough for him? Or–chills ripple through my aching body at the thought–did the critic publish his review today and send Chef Fontaine into a fresh rage?

A big, cowardly part of me wants to stay safely under this pillow and never face that man again. I know he has every right to be mad; I know I deserve every lecture he might give. But seeing his look of icy disdain last night…

It broke something inside me. I like him so much, *admire* him so much, and he looked at me like dirt on his shoe. I can't face that again. I can't.

And yet the Beast is still here, knocking steadily at my door like he's prepared to stay out in that hallway all night. Like he brought snacks and drinks and a fold-out chair, and he's ready to outlast me.

"Okay." He can't hear me. *I* can barely hear my hoarse, reedy voice, but for some reason I keep mumbling. "Okay, okay. 'M coming."

My stomach lurches as I sit up, swinging my legs out of bed. The bedroom tilts from side to side like a ship cabin in a storm, and I have to lean one hand on the wall for balance as I stagger into the hall.

Knock. Knock. Knock. "Miss Fray?"

"I'm coming," I call, louder this time. The knocking stops.

My breaths are ragged as I make it to the front door, slumping one shoulder against the wooden frame. I scrabble at the lock, my fingers numb and fumbling, and when I finally tug the door open, I'm faint with the effort.

"Holy shit."

The rumble of his voice makes me tingle, and I stare at Chef Fontaine's shoes. He's wearing battered leather boots under his chef's pants–like he's a biker, not a fancy French chef–and they're planted in my hallway like he never plans to move.

"Miss Fray? Chloe."

Sweat beads my upper lip, and I screw one eye shut as I raise my gaze. It drags slowly up his long legs, his muscled thighs, his solid stomach and big chest and the open collar at his throat–

Chef Fontaine stares at me, cheeks pale behind his short, brown beard. He swallows, and the thick column of his throat bobs, the collar of his white chef's jacket open wide enough to show a plain gray t-shirt and a dusting of chest hair.

I frown at the hollow of his throat, focusing every last brain cell on not toppling over.

"Hi, Chef Fontaine. Is there…" I trail off, licking my lips as I force my spinning brain to concentrate. "Do you need my signature on something?"

Please leave. Please get whatever you need and go.

This man, the man I've harbored a terrible crush on for months, already saw me at my lowest last night. He already lost all faith in me—and let everyone within a half-mile radius know it.

Now he's here again, and I'm dressed in baggy yellow pinstripe pajamas, and there is a very real risk I might hurl on his snowy white jacket. There's no other explanation: the damn universe is kicking me while I'm down.

"I came to make sure you got home okay last night." Chef Fontaine speaks quietly, but his voice carries easily. It settles into my brain, soothing my racing thoughts, even as I blink at him. He did what?

"Um." I try for a smile, but it feels more like a grimace. "I got home fine, obviously. Thank you."

"Please understand, if I had known you were ill…" The Beast trails off, and his thunderous scowl makes his nickname suit him for once. "I would not have sent you out like that, Chloe. I would have ensured you got home safely."

Huh. Guess I'm not the only person who woke up filled with shame. His is unnecessary, though.

"Noted." I try to raise a thumbs up, then snatch for the door frame when the room lurches again. "I know you're not a bad man, Chef. You didn't need to come here to tell me that. Especially since I don't work for you anymore."

"I didn't come here to *tell* you that." He sounds offended. "I came to show you, Chloe. Will you let me in?"

Oh. Oh yeah. We're standing in my doorway. Or *he's* standing and I'm slumping, squinting at Chef Fontaine out of one eye and thinking dizzily that he's the most handsome man

I've ever seen.

The Beast blinks. A flush spreads over his cheekbones. Shoot, did I say that bit out loud?

"Yes," my ex-boss rumbles. "You did." But he doesn't seem mad about it—he seems downright pleased, the corner of his mouth curling up, and when he nudges past me into my apartment, he takes my hand in a steadying hold.

"I'm going to help you, Chloe. You need someone to look after you tonight. Are you going to argue with me on this?"

I let him lead me through my own rooms, a giddy grin spreading over my hot cheeks. "Ha! Nope. No, sir."

Because maybe this is real, and Chef Fontaine is really here, or maybe this is a vertigo-induced daydream. Either way, I'm no fool, not about him. You couldn't pay me millions to send this man away.

* * *

"Fresh air and hot soup." Chef Fontaine whips my bedroom curtains open with a flourish, letting in the pink rays of sunset. I tug the bed covers over my lap, watching him as I get comfy against the headboard, sucking in big lungfuls of the cool air wafting through the cracked window. My racing heart settles.

The room doesn't spin quite so badly as long as I'm staring at him. That's my excuse and I'm sticking to it.

"The title of your album?"

His stern mouth twitches. "My professional recommendation."

"I had no idea you went to medical school."

The Beast turns and levels me a *look*. Standing in front of my bedroom windows, silhouetted against the pink sky, he looks even burlier and grumpier than usual. Like an angry god in a chef's jacket.

I bite my lip, squeezing handfuls of bed covers in my lap. He fired me. He *fired* me. I can't forget that. But it's so hard to feel properly wary of Chef Fontaine when he strides out of my bedroom and returns with a glass of cool water; when he places a box of painkillers on my nightstand with a pointed look.

"In case you have a headache."

"Thank you." He's so *close*. After months of only seeing him across a busy kitchen or past the heads and shoulders of a crowd, Chef Fontaine is leaning over my bed to plump my pillows, and I wouldn't even need to straighten my arm to touch him.

I could smell him. Could flatten a palm over his chest; feel the steady *thump, thump, thump* of his heartbeat, slow and relentless like his knock on my door.

Instead, I squeeze the bed sheets tighter, and close my eyes against the rush of dizziness swooping up my spine.

"Chloe?"

Fingertips graze my cheek, the touch so quick and light that maybe I dreamed it. I tilt my head, and there he is again. A warm, dry palm cupping my cheek. Cradling me like something precious.

"I'm okay." My tongue darts out, wetting my bottom lip, and Chef Fontaine makes a low noise. "I'm just dizzy. It's okay."

A tongue clicks. "Lie back."

Ha. Do you know how many times I've longed to hear a command like that in the Beast's low voice? I melt obediently against the pillows, grinning.

"What's funny?"

I huff a laugh and tug the covers up to my neck. "Nothing."

"Chloe."

"It's really nothing."

"*Chloe.* Tell me."

I shrug, and I don't know what the hell I'm thinking when I blurt out an honest answer. The vertigo must be messing with my brain; it must have short-circuited my sense of self-preservation. "I just like when you're bossy, Chef. That's all."

Silence.

Awkward silence, stretching tense and horrible between us. And I'm wincing, wishing I'd never answered my door to him, when Chef Fontaine's thumb starts moving over my cheek again.

Back and forth. Back and forth. Gentle swoops of his thumb, his hands so much bigger than mine. These hands butcher meat and wield cleavers; they're brutal and skilled and scarred.

"Is there someone I could call? To come and look after you."

"I don't need—"

"That's not what I asked." Finally, I risk squinting one eye open again. My bedroom is washed pink by the sunset, and Chef Fontaine is shadowed as he leans over my bed.

"The doctor said it would go away on its own. I just need to wait it out."

The Beast shifts, and the floorboards creak under his bulk. "Alone?"

When I shrug, my vision blurs. "I guess."

I don't get taken care of. Ever, really. With my friends, my family, my neighbors, *everyone*, I'm the caretaker. I'm the one they rely on, and I hate to admit it, but… it's one-sided. When I'm down and out, there's radio silence.

"No." He's grumpy again, an edge to his voice, but rather

than making me nervous, I feel all... warm. "That is not happening. I will stay with you until you are well again. With your permission, of course," he adds, sounding even more surly. As though he thinks I'm about to send him away.

Hardly. If I weren't so freaking dizzy, I'd tackle him in a hug. He's my grumpy ex-boss, the *Beast*, and he publicly fired me yesterday, and yet I don't remember the last time I experienced someone else's concern.

I feel safe with him.

Cared for.

It's kind of pathetic, but hey, I'm sick. If I can't be tragic now, then when can I?

"You said something about soup."

The shadow in my bedroom tips his head back and laughs. It's a low sound, rumbling and rich, and it tingles over every inch of my body. I don't even want to imagine how much it would cost to hire Chef Fontaine for a private meal, and I'm sure as hell not offering, but he chuckles again and pushes to his feet.

The floorboards groan. Inhaling steadily, I tip my head back to watch him staring down at me.

"What ingredients do you have?"

Another shrug. He scoffs.

"You worked in a kitchen, Chloe."

I ignore his use of the past tense, even though it pinches in my chest. "Yeah. As a *server*."

Another grumble, too quiet for me to make out, and then he's striding from my bedroom, footsteps echoing down the hall. I lean my head back against the pillows, blinking up at the crack on my ceiling. The room's spinning less than earlier. Already, the fresh air is helping.

I don't call and tell him that, obviously. Chef Fontaine is too far away to hear, and besides, I'd be crazy to turn down a meal from him.

After all, I don't work in his restaurant anymore. After tonight, I'll probably never see him again.

Matthieu

The knife slices through bulbous white onions, the blade damnably blunt. I grimace, mentally sharpening the edge, but for all my grousing, I feel better already. Relaxed.

This is what I'm good at. A kitchen is where I feel most sure. Certain of my place in the world and what I can offer, including what I can offer the beautiful young woman in the other room.

The woman I fired. I'd do well to remember that. Chloe may be sweet and forgiving, she may be glad of my help while she's ill, but that doesn't mean she'll ever want to see me again.

"Come on, you blunt bastard," I mutter to the knife, chopping rhythmically into the wooden board. Perfect slivers of white onion pile up beside my hand, and this is definitely overkill for the simple stew I'm making, but I can't help it.

Once you set your sights on perfection, it's impossible to aim for less. The pursuit is addictive.

Perfection.

That word conjures many images to mind. The glossy red skin of a ripe apple; the slick slide of melting butter across a frying pan. The sucking pull of a thick risotto, sticking to a wooden spoon as I stir the rice.

And Chloe Fray's husky voice.

Her bottomless brown eyes.

The roller-coaster outline of her curves, only hinted at beneath her baggy pin-striped pajamas.

I curse and dab my forehead with my wrist. It doesn't matter. I've got no business thinking of her that way. First she was my employee and off limits; now, there's an uncrossable gulf between us. One gouged out with ruined careers and harsh words.

But no matter. Pulling a chipped blue bowl from the cupboard, I plate up her vegetable stew like I'm serving royalty: with a sprig of fresh basil and a bright lemon wedge, and a hunk of torn, crusty bread for dipping.

"Try and sit up if you can." Chloe's bedroom is cooler with the window open, the faint sounds of traffic drifting up from the street. She's flicked her bedside lamp on, and it casts a golden glow.

"That smells... *wow*." She scrambles up to lean against the headboard, one eye still screwed shut but her face flushed with more color than earlier. "How much would this cost me in Chez Fontaine?"

"Before or after the review comes out?"

It's a bad joke. I regret the words as soon as they leave my mouth. Chloe flinches, her shoulders sagging inside her pajamas, and I settle the tray on her lap, stealing another greedy brush of fingertips along her cheek.

"It doesn't matter now. Forget it, Chloe." My voice is gruff, but she manages a smile for me. Brave girl. I watch her closely, heart thumping against my ribs.

The mattress squeals as I sit awkwardly on the bed by her feet. They're two small lumps, buried under the covers, and I'm not thinking as I reach out, one hand settling on the nearest foot and kneading it through the fabric.

"*Mmph*." Chloe makes a startled noise, but she doesn't pull away, and when I glance up, she smiles around a mouthful of stew. Her foot nudges my hip, and I change my grip, holding her tighter.

This is so messed up. She must hate me, but I can't stop. I *won't* stop, not until she sends me away. Seeing her like this, with her curly dark hair piled in a messy bun, a healthy glow creeping over her brown cheeks–I'm settled. All the nerves and bitterness that have been gnawing at my insides since I fired her, they just… fade away.

I'm a professional chef. A man of great appetites.

But looking at Chloe now, I'm learning about an entirely different sort of hunger.

"It's getting late." I tilt my head toward the dark windows, the first stars winking in the navy sky. "How are you feeling? Any better?"

Chloe watches me steadily, blowing on a spoon of stew. She certainly *looks* a lot better. Less dizzy and pale. And though it makes me an asshole, part of me hopes she's not completely well yet. That she'll need me around for a few hours longer.

As though she reads my mind, Chloe's mouth quirks up on one side. "I feel terrible, Chef Fontaine."

"Matthieu."

The smile grows. "*Matthieu*. I feel like I'm at death's door. I may not make it to morning. Perhaps you could stay the

163

night?"

She's clearly joking, but I nod anyway. "If you insist, Miss Fray."

"Chloe. And I do."

Good. *Good.* We've only had a simple conversation, but my heart's pounding like I've sprinted a mile. The thought of leaving her, of going back out onto that cold, lonely street, of facing the reality of that review...

"I'll take the sofa," I rasp.

Chloe nods slowly, sipping another spoonful of stew. Her pleased hum makes my cock twitch, and she murmurs, "If you insist."

Fucking hell.

She's *ill*. She has vertigo, damn it. I scrub a hand down my face, lecturing myself silently. Chloe Fray is not mine to want.

Keep it in your pants, asshole.

* * *

I clean the dishes and open the windows. Water Chloe's plants and reshelve a messy stack of books in her small living room. I even put a load of towels in the laundry before finally forcing myself to stop.

It's just... addictive. Taking care of Chloe Fray. Who knew I could get such a high from cooking soup for a woman? From tidying her apartment and restocking her fridge; bringing her hot ginger tea and cooling her forehead with a damp cloth?

You'd think my nickname was Mother Theresa, not the Beast. But when she smiles weakly at me from her nest in the bed and tells me for the dozenth time that she's feeling a little better, I'm so triumphant I could punch the air.

Seriously. Who the fuck am I?

"Mm." Chloe hums after sipping from her mug—the third hot drink I've brought her in an hour. I'm like a damn puppy, bringing her gifts in exchange for a smile. "Honey and lemon?"

"Yes." I linger at her bedside, scratching the back of my neck. "In case you have a sore throat."

Outside, the sky's inky black, and the windows of the city are lit up gold. It's late, even for restaurant workers. Well past midnight. Shit, should Chloe be sleeping?

"Are you tired?"

Chloe shakes her head with a smile. She's doing that more freely now than a few hours ago—before, she'd get visibly dizzy, screwing her eyes shut. But now, her eyes are bright and focused, and her cheeks are a healthy brown.

"I should hit the sofa. Let you get some sleep."

"Okay. Goodnight, Matthieu."

"Yes. Goodnight."

I stride out of her bedroom, cursing the deflated feeling in my chest. What did I think would happen? That she'd flip back the covers and tell me to crawl into bed? Idiot.

An hour later, I'm wide awake, staring at the shadows shifting over the living room ceiling. Chloe's sofa is lumpy and far shorter than my body, my knees dangling over one end, and I can't fucking sleep when I'm on edge like this.

I'm hard.

Fuck, I'm such an asshole. I offered to stay and care for this woman, and now I'm *hard*. Lying here on her sofa, glaring up at her white ceiling, my body primed like I have a shot in hell with Chloe Fray. I kicked off my boots and tossed my chef's jacket over a nearby chair, but that's all I dared to take off. I clearly don't need to give myself ideas.

"Asshole," I mutter, wincing as I shift around, trying to get comfortable. "You are a very sick man."

"Are you?" Her husky voice makes me jump. Chloe stands in the shadowed doorway, arms hugging her waist. Those baggy pajama pants pool around her feet, but I catch a glimpse of bare, painted toes, scrunching against the floorboards. "Why are you sick, Chef Fontaine?"

I frown at her little plump form. Is this a dream? Her messy bun has slid to one side, and escaped curls frame her cheeks. She looks perfect. Tailor-made to drive me insane.

"I want things I shouldn't."

Chloe pads closer. "Everyone does that."

"Do they?"

"Yeah."

The sofa groans as I sit up, clumsy and squinting in the darkness. Chloe's so quiet, I can barely hear her breathing.

When I pat the sofa cushion beside me, it's a test of sorts. I want to make sure she's real, and if she is, I want to try my luck. See how much she trusts me after all.

The cushion dips under her weight. "I was going to the kitchen." She leans forward, the fabric of her pajamas shifting over her skin, and there's a dull thud against the coffee table. An empty glass. "Fetching some water."

"Oh." I roll my neck, pushing away my dismay. Why the hell did I stop her? "I'd have done that for you."

"I know. But I'm feeling much better. I'm barely dizzy at all."

I wait for her to leave, to go and get a drink like she said. But there's only silence between us, expectant and heavy.

Finally, I can't bear it anymore. I need to ask her. "What do you want that you shouldn't, Chloe?"

She hums and settles back against the cushions like she was waiting for a cue. Like she's getting comfy, settling in for a while, and fuck, I hope so. She smells delicious—like fresh linen and rose.

I grab the blanket I borrowed and settle it over her lap. Chloe burrows into it, then says, "Lots of things, really."

"Such as?"

"More money," she says flatly, and I can't help my rough laugh. Chloe is so forthright, and it's refreshing—like the cool breeze filtering through the open window. "More sleep. Fancy kitchen appliances. Money to pay a cleaner. One of those fancy leather bound journals and a set of really nice pens."

I wait, mouth dry, as she spills more of her soul for me.

"A vacation. A bubble bath. A cooking class."

A cooking class? I could give her that. And there's a bathtub at my place, and I could take her away somewhere, and—

Chloe blows out a hard breath. "A new job, obviously."

Right. I close my mouth with a click. With almost every single thing on her list, I've made her life harder. But Chloe's watching me now out of the corner of her eye, so still and careful in the gloom.

"Those aren't bad things to want," I force myself to say. Because I can't just hire her again because I find her attractive. That would be pretty fucking low of me, and I don't *want* Chloe working for me again, disastrous night with the critic aside.

I want more from her. I want *everything*.

If she could ever want a big, grumpy bastard like me, anyway.

"I'll give you a strong reference," I offer instead. And I expect her scorn, but instead Chloe smiles so wide, I can see it in the dark.

"Thank you, Matthieu. That will help me so much."

"Sure. Of course."

God, this is awkward. Should I leave? Should I fetch her that water? Should I thunder across her living room and leap out of that window?

"There's one more thing on my list." Chloe's elbow nudges me, and I jolt. Her list? Right, yeah. Her *things-she-shouldn't-want* list. Bathtubs and cooking classes.

"What's that?"

Maybe I can get it for her, too.

There's a pause, then Chloe murmurs, "A kiss from Chef Fontaine."

168

Chloe

~∾⊙∾~

Well. Here goes nothing. What's a girl to do when a man fires her, then turns up at her apartment and makes her the most delicious stew she's ever tasted?

Shoot her shot, obviously. It's not like I have anything to lose. And besides, I've wanted the man currently crowding my sofa for *so freaking long.* I've had naughty dreams about Chef Fontaine. I've stared at him so often, I know the laughter lines on his face by heart. The last time I got my haircut, I sat in that stupid chair, wondering if *he'd* like it.

And after tonight, I may never see him again. So it's now or never.

Time to be brave.

"A kiss from Chef Fontaine." My words land between us with a clang. Matthieu stiffens, turning to stone beside me. A gorgeous, burly, impossible statue.

"Or not," I mutter, humiliation burning my cheeks. Shoot my shot? What the hell was I thinking? I lurch to my feet, a sudden wave of dizziness making me stagger to the side. My hip bumps his knee, and then Matthieu comes back to life, pulling me down to sit on his lap before I know what's happening. "What are you—"

"You want a kiss, no?"

He's so freaking French. Holy crap, this man is hot.

"Yes, but—only if you *want* to. Like, really want to."

"Chloe?" His breath is warm on my neck. Oh god. "I want to. I really, *really* want to."

Good. Great. Perfect. That's... that is very good news, and it's only occurring to me now that I barely know what I'm doing. I mean, I've seen kisses in movies and I've read books and stuff; I know the general idea. But it's a lot more intimidating when you find yourself cradled in the lap of a giant, grumpy chef, especially one whose spicy, manly scent makes your heart stutter.

"I'm still fired, right?" My feet bounce nervously against his leg. Weirdly, I hope so. I don't want this to be something gross.

Matthieu nods, his handsome face etched in a scowl. "I am afraid so, yes."

"Phew." I grin at him, relieved, and even in the gloom, I can see his surprise. "Let's do this, then. Um. Whenever you're ready."

Whenever you're ready. God, how lame. But Matthieu doesn't tease me for it: he shifts me in his lap, then cradles the side of my jaw. The big pad of his thumb swoops over my skin, and my lips part like magic. Open sesame.

"You are a beautiful woman," Matthieu murmurs, and he's frowning like he's mad about it. "The most beautiful woman I've ever seen."

I snort. "Yeah, right." Somehow, dressed in my baggy pin-striped pajamas, I doubt that.

But when his hazel eyes bore into mine, so intense in the moonlight... I believe him. He really means it. And woah, that's a rush.

I feel powerful. Confident. I'm like a whole different person as I loop an arm around his neck. I'm not even embarrassed when I tell him I've never done this before–kissing, touching, you name it. I've always been too busy, working and caring for everyone else.

Chef Fontaine growls, pleased and possessive.

"Good. You are mine."

Yup. That works for me, especially when he tilts my head back and brushes his lips over my cheek, the tiny contact sending heat rippling down my spine. Matthieu drops gentle, barely-there kisses on my forehead, my temple, the tip of my nose and the point of my chin.

Every kiss scorches down to my soul.

Every possessive rumble makes my pulse tick faster, my heart rattling in my chest. I'm squirming in his lap, breathless and needy, and when he reaches my mouth, he doesn't kiss me like I expect–he drags my bottom lip between his teeth and gives a sharp nip.

Oh.

I sway in his lap with a moan. I'm dizzy again, but for a whole new reason. A *delicious* reason. Chef Fontaine has addled my senses; the Beast has caught me in his fangs.

A warm tongue swipes where he bit me, soothing the sting. I scrabble at his shoulders, wanting more, wanting *him*, wanting to get closer. He could kiss me forever and I'd still beg for more.

Finally, finally, his lips slant against mine. We're joined, pressed together, sharing breaths and body heat. When I flatten my palm over the soft gray t-shirt clinging to Matthieu's chest, his heart calls out to me.

Thump. Thump. Thump.

It's beating fast. He's affected by this, too, and I'm so tragically relieved by that. Even if my kissing skills are unpolished, he wants me.

"Chloe." Matthieu kisses me again, harder. Deeper. *Thump, thump, thump,* goes his heart against my palm, and his tongue slides against mine, then pulls away. "Fuck. Lovely girl. I shouldn't do this while you are ill."

"Yes, you should." I tug at his shirt, pulling him closer. We're flattened together, seamless, and it's still not enough. It will never be enough. "You definitely should."

His laugh sounds broken, and I almost laugh too, but then he's leaning back. Pulling away. Cool air washes over the front of my pajamas, and I shiver, nipples already hard under the fabric.

"Come on." There's no room for argument in his tone. "I'll get you that water. Then you're going to bed."

* * *

I sleep through my alarm, and when I wake up, Matthieu is gone. There's almost no sign of him in the apartment, and if it weren't for the open windows and the slight dip on the sofa cushions, I might think I hallucinated him last night.

Did that *really* happen?

Did my ex-boss come here, cook me stew, then kiss me breathless on the sofa?

172

Yeesh.

My steps are clumsy as I move through my apartment, but at least I'm not dizzy anymore. The walls aren't spinning; the floor's not tilting. The mid-morning sounds of the street aren't weirdly muffled in my ears.

I'm better. So... that's good.

God, how can I miss him already?

There's a note on my kitchen table, and I lunge for it like a starving woman. It's written in a strong, surprisingly loopy script, and says simply: *Hope you feel better this morning. Here is my number—call if you need anything. Matthieu.*

I read it over and over, tracing the words with my thumb, but after the third time, some of the glowy feeling in my chest fades away.

Call if you need anything. That's what the note says. Not: *call me*, period. Not: *I'll come back later.*

Will I ever see him again?

No. *No.* I am not this girl–I don't moon around my apartment, pining after a man when there are real problems to fix. Not even a gorgeous, surly, perfect man like Chef Fontaine.

Ugh. I need to find a job. But first, I stomp through to my living room and lever open my battered laptop on the coffee table. It doesn't take long to find the critic's office address in the city, and after a short pause, I scrawl it on the paper below Matthieu's note.

I can't save a scrap of paper like I'm starting a shrine to my ex-boss.

Honestly. I need to keep *some* dignity.

Matthieu

My head is buried in my hands when my desk phone rings, jolting me upright in my chair. The office door is open, and shouts of laughter and strains of the radio float through from the ongoing kitchen clean up. It's like another world through that doorway. A happier, carefree one.

I glare at the ringing phone, a headache pounding in my ears. All my bad decisions are squeezing my skull this morning: kissing Chloe; starting a stupid restaurant; staying awake all night with my body craving a woman asleep in her room.

A woman I *fired*. Who I have no intention of rehiring. What the hell was I thinking?

Chloe will hate me once she's well again.

"Yes?" I growl.

I do not have a beautiful phone manner. Not even on a good day. But the voice that echoes down the line is enough to make even *my* throat tight and my palms damp.

"Chef Fontaine?"

It's him—I'd know his voice anywhere. The critic. The man who will destroy my career any day now.

"What is this?" I scowl at the open doorway. The handset creaks in my grip. "A courtesy call?"

"Something like that."

Fuck. I knew it was coming, but it's still a kick to the gut. The restaurant won't close from one bad review, not right away, but this will set us on a different path. One without Michelin stars, that's for sure. And I can't look away from the open kitchen doorway; from the sight of Pablo leaning against a counter, his head tipped back as he laughs at something one of the pot washes said.

This will hurt him. It will hurt all of my staff. They've worked so hard for so long, and now it's all ruined.

It's my fault. All of it. Chloe may have spilled the food, but I'm the boss.

It all comes back to me.

"I'd like to come again."

Now *that* gives me pause. I blink, my tired brain trying desperately to keep up.

"You—why would you want that?"

There's a soft laugh and a rustle of clothing down the line. Then: "I had a visit at my office this morning. A young woman begging me to give your restaurant another chance. Apparently I shouldn't hold her throwing food over my person against you."

Chloe.

Fuck. What was she doing out in the city?

"Was she alright?" I sound like I've swallowed gravel. "Did she look dizzy?"

Another chuckle. "You are both rather concerned for each

other. Tell me: if I come again, will she be the one serving me? I only have a finite wardrobe, you understand."

"No." I swallow hard. He didn't answer me, damn it. Was she okay or not? "No. After last time, I fired her."

The long pause makes a flush prickle over my skin. "Ah." The critic's voice is light. "Perhaps it's churlish of me, but as a diner, I have to say I'm relieved. Shall I return this evening, then?"

My heart thumps hard enough to bruise. "Please do."

It's strangely quiet as I hang up the phone, my fingers numb and my eyes dry. The radio still hums in the kitchen, but the sound warps in my ears.

It's happening–a second chance. And it's all thanks to Chloe Fray.

* * *

Two days later, I'm checking ingredients in the walk-in freezer when I hear her husky voice. It's soft, so quiet that I think maybe I'm going crazy, but then I hear Pablo say something in reply, their voices drifting past as they walk to my office.

She's *here*.

Chloe's here.

After everything that happened… I didn't think I'd hear from her again. I called her after the second visit from the critic, riding high on the triumph of a flawless night, but she didn't pick up the phone.

I swore to myself I'd take the hint. But when I hear her voice, I lunge out of the freezer like a madman.

"… Left it on his desk, hang on," Pablo's saying. He ducks inside my office, and Chloe loiters in the doorway, gripping the strap of her tote bag tightly like it's a lifeline. Even from behind, I can tell she's feeling better. Dressed in a cream sweater and jeans, she's standing straighter with her shoulders back, her dark curls teased into a knot at her nape.

What I wouldn't give to tug that tie from her hair. To finger comb the long dresses down her back; to lift a lock and press it to my nose, breathing her scent in.

Chloe murmurs something, and I don't hear the words, but I catch my name. She starts to call me Matthieu, then corrects herself to Chef Fontaine.

Well. That's as good an excuse as any to interrupt.

"Perhaps I can help." I touch her shoulder, and she spins around, eyes wide. Chloe stares up at me, her posture suddenly tense, and my heart sinks.

She's only relaxed with Pablo, then. Not with me.

"No," she blurts, confirming my fears. "No, we've got it, thanks. I'm just here for my last paycheck, and then I'll get out of your way."

I scowl. "You're not in the way. You could never be in the way."

Pablo makes a surprised grunt in my office, then emerges with a small envelope pinched between his fingers.

"Here you go, Chloe." He's talking to her, but looking at me. Seeing right through me, the bastard, one eyebrow raised. "Thanks for dropping in."

"Sure." She takes the envelope gingerly and tucks it in her pocket. "Thank you."

God. This is awkward. Is it always this awkward after I've fired someone? No, I don't think so—I'm not usually desperate for them to stay a few minutes longer. I'm not usually fighting the urge to grab their elbow and march them inside my office, keeping their soothing presence all to myself.

Fighting the urge–and losing. Chloe makes a surprised noise when I take her elbow, but she doesn't fight me as I steer her through the doorway, nudging the door shut behind us. It closes on Pablo's knowing smirk with a thump.

"You're here." That's me: Matthieu Fontaine. Master of the obvious. "You got me a second chance with the critic."

A flush creeps over her cheeks. "It was the least I could do." Damn it, why won't she look at me? Chloe's brown eyes are darting all over the office, settling everywhere except my face. "I'm the one who blew your shot the first time around."

"You were ill."

Chloe shrugs, still staring over my shoulder. "I shouldn't have come in to work."

"No, you shouldn't have. But–"

"Did it go well? Your second chance?"

I frown at her. *Look at me, lovely girl.* "Yes. It went well."

She blows out a slow breath, and for the first time since she noticed me, her shoulders relax an inch. And when Chloe's eyes dart to mine quickly, then away, she looks *nervous*. Like she didn't sit in my lap only a few days ago. Like she didn't ask me to kiss her in that warm, husky voice.

"Chloe?"

"Hm?"

I graze my fingertips over her cheek. I never claimed to be a good man, and a possessive thrill snakes through me when she finally meets my eyes. *Yes.* This is when the world feels right: when Chloe's eyes are on me, and mine are on her. "Are you feeling better now?"

She nods, gazing up at me, pearly teeth digging into her plump bottom lip. Fuck, I want this woman so badly–and I know, suddenly, that if I don't show her that now, I'll never get the chance again.

She's mine.

She's *mine*, damn it.

She let me pull her onto my lap. Let me kiss her deeply, *hungrily*, her tongue stroking against mine.

"Chloe," I rasp, moving closer and watching as her pupils blow wide. "Lovely girl. Don't you want to kiss me anymore?"

Chloe

‧❦‧

"Don't you want to kiss me anymore?"

I stare at Chef Fontaine, and shocked laughter bubbles up my throat. How can he even think that? I'd swap a kidney to kiss this man again.

"It's not that."

Oh, gosh. His smile is so kind. His hazel eyes crinkle at the corners, and his beard shifts as he smiles down at me, watching. Waiting. So patient, even now, with the bangs and clatters of the kitchen floating through his office door, and no doubt a million things demanding his attention.

"I, um." I wet my lip, searching for the words. "I figured you're busy. And that I've caused you enough trouble. And that you probably–you probably regret kissing me before."

Because Matthieu *left*. While I was sleeping, without saying goodbye. And that note he left me was sweet, but it didn't seem like he really wanted to hear from me again.

So I moved on. Or distracted myself, anyway, first smoothing things out with the critic and then sending out dozens of job applications. Since this man stole out of my apartment like a thief in the night, I've kept busy and resolved never to bother him again.

Even though my heart throbs whenever I think of him.

Even though my lips tingle every time I close my eyes and relive that kiss, my arms wrapped tight around my waist.

"I do not regret it." Even his kind words come out in a growl. I bite my lip, gazing up at him, hardly daring to breathe as I wait for more. "It was... you were perfect, Chloe. Your lips were the best thing I've ever tasted."

Coming from a top chef, I guess that's saying something.

"I, um." God, he's seen me dizzy and rumpled in my pajamas, and I'm *still* nervous around him. "Does that mean... can we do it again?"

I have places to be, too. A thousand things to do. Calls to make and groceries to pick up for my neighbor. An apartment to clean. But all those mental To Do lists and external worries melt away when Chef Fontaine steps forward, resting both big palms on the sides of my neck.

His hands are warm and dry. When I swallow, he traces his thumb over my throat.

"I'm going to kiss you now, Chloe." I nod, that thumb trailing up to my chin, and Matthieu keeps talking in that deep, rumbly voice that thrills all the way to my core. "But this time, I will not stop kissing you. Not today, not ever."

Holy crap. I stare up at him, unblinking, and pinch the side of my wrist.

I'm definitely awake.

"If we do this, lovely girl, you are mine. Do you understand? You are mine and I am yours. Nod if you agree."

I tip my chin, head spinning. Matthieu growls and ducks

his head, sealing his mouth against mine.

Heat.

Spice.

The decadent slide of his tongue.

I forget to breathe for a long moment, and when I finally remember to suck in a lungful of air, my hands jerk up, clinging to Matthieu's shoulders. He's so big and broad; his chest and belly brush against my front. He's *solid*, immovable, like a great storm could rage at the city and buildings would fall and he'd still be standing here. Inevitable.

I'm not a small girl. I'm short, sure, but there's more than a handful on my hips, my waist, my breasts. Next to Chef Fontaine, though, I'm positively dainty, and that sends a delicious shiver over my skin.

"Chloe." When Matthieu tears his mouth away, resting his forehead against mine, he sounds winded too. Knocked sideways. "Beautiful girl. Lovely girl. Will you let me taste you?"

Taste me?

Isn't he already doing that?

I open my mouth to point that out, but Chef Fontaine's already turned away, spinning the lock on his door. And when he turns back and guides me across his office to lean against the edge of his desk, his eyes are so hungry that I snap my mouth closed.

Whatever he's talking about, I want it. Even when he rubs his thumbs over my hips. Even when he reaches between us and pops the top button of my jeans.

"What are you–*oh.*" I tilt my head back, eyes drifting closed, as his thick fingers nudge inside my underwear, sliding through my slick folds.

"Do you really not know?" Amusement laces his words.

My mouth twitches. I keep my eyes closed, heart pounding.

"I guess I have an idea."

"I think you do."

I could stop him. I know that, as surely as I know my own name. This man would never force me into a single thing–the very thought of it would make him sick. I *know* that, so when I bite my lip, keeping quiet, I'm breathless with wanting him to keep going.

And Chef Fontaine does not disappoint. Those skilled fingers swirl over my clit; they probe deeper inside my panties with such possessiveness that my whole body flushes hot. He coils the tension in my belly tighter and tighter, playing me so confidently with just the swirl of his fingertips, and I'm bucking against his hand, gasping for air, shaking and trembling and dizzy all over again–

"Oh!" My eyes snap open wide. Matthieu watches me, triumphant eyes burning as I shudder against his fingers, heat flooding my body in waves.

I've never done that before. Not with someone else. And on my own, it's never been so overwhelming, so perfect, so *much*.

"More?" Matthieu pulls his hand away carefully, holding my gaze as he slips each finger into his mouth one by one. His cheeks hollow, and lord, he's tasting me, just like he said. It's so wrong, so twisted, and I love it.

"Uh-huh." I nod so hard my neck twinges. "More. Please."

Something clatters over his desk as he boosts me up to sit. A cup of pens, maybe. Then my jeans are peeled down in a blur, my underwear following straight after, and I don't even have time to be embarrassed by my faded pink cotton panties before Matthieu presses my thighs wide. He falls to his knees between my legs with an almighty thump, and he waits until I'm watching him, his thumbs tracing circles on my knees.

"Are you ready, Chloe?"

Born ready. Oh my god.

His mouth quirks up at the corner, and then he's leaning forward, his shoulders forcing my legs further apart.

* * *

I've seen this man taste famous delicacies in his kitchen. I've seen him try the freshest, most delicious ingredients, and I've heard him groan when he samples the perfect dish from visiting chefs. When Matthieu tastes something he loves, his eyes drift closed and his chest puffs up, and it's like watching something sacred, seeing this man eat.

That's what I thought before, anyway. But now I know better—now I've seen the primal hunger in his eyes when he licks between my legs.

"Chloe." His low voice rumbles against my core, vibrating and tingling everywhere. He licks me once, twice, *deeper*. "You taste like perfection. The sweetest dessert."

My breath catches, and I squeeze the edge of the desk so hard the wood creaks. It's so hot, so wet, so *intense.*

Matthieu shuffles closer on his knees, sliding two hands beneath me and gripping my ass with both palms. He kneads me, lifts me closer, tilts me higher, won't let me escape by even an inch, and I'm helpless, being devoured by him.

"Oh my—oh my *god.*"

Matthieu grunts. He buries his tongue deep inside me, and the tip of his nose rubs against my clit, side to side. I moan, loud and broken, and I'd be embarrassed about that, would worry about the kitchen workers, except this is too much. I can't think of anything but how this feels.

It feels decadent.

Naughty.

So wrong and so right. A stolen moment with a man who shouldn't be mine. Except… why shouldn't he? And why shouldn't I be his? What does it matter that Chef Fontaine fired me, when together, we can feel like *this*?

"Mat–Matthieu!"

I can barely wheeze out his name.

This time when I come, my legs clamp against his shoulders. I squeeze him tight, like some primal, instinctive part of me doesn't want to let him escape, and I moan at his office ceiling, ragged and broken.

I've barely slumped back against the desk before he's standing again. Pushing closer between my thighs, hands fumbling at the button of his pants.

"Please," Matthieu grinds out, and thank god I'm not the only one who's breathless. "Let me inside you, Chloe. Please. I can't stand it. Please."

I never thought I'd hear Chef Fontaine beg for *anything*, but this? It sends a burst of heat and longing and power rippling through my core.

"Uh-huh." My hands join his, scrabbling at his button. I need that too. I need him now. And he doesn't disappoint, his cock pushing inside me, warm and thick, and so hard that my eyes nearly cross. I grab two fistfuls of his crisp, white chef's jacket, and cling on for dear life as Matthieu thrusts deeper, *deeper*, then starts to pound between my legs.

He's not gentle.

I don't want him to be.

I don't *need* him to be, not after he made me come twice already. What I want, what I desperately need, is the full force of his hunger for me. The slam of his hips, bruising against my inner thighs; his hot breath on my cheek; his white-knuckled grip on my ass. It's brutal and it's tender and it's so freaking perfect, and the little grunts we both make are animalistic. We sound like we're out of our minds.

"*Chloe.* Fuck."

I want him to say my name like that every time. Like I'm breaking him. Like I'm hollowing out his insides.

"Yes," I hiss. "Do it. Take me hard, Matthieu."

His cock slams into me, impossibly faster. It's a vicious blur, an onslaught of sensations. But his big body's so overwhelming against mine, and something's pressing against my clit, and I can't breathe, I can't *breathe.*

I come with a squeak. With my jaw locked open, and my toes curling behind his back. Then Matthieu groans like the Beast he's named after, and wet warmth floods my core.

Mine.

He's mine. The proof's dripping onto the surface of his desk.

Even as the distant sounds of the kitchen fade back in, and our ragged breaths slow down, and cooling sweat prickles on my skin–that's all I can think.

Matthieu Fontaine is mine. The Beast is finally mine.

And I'm his.

Matthieu

One year later

Like most nights, I'm the last person to leave Chez Fontaine. The last one standing. The kitchen is so clean it sparkles, the dining tables are ghostly silent, and there's no one left here but me.

My footsteps echo as I stride through the restaurant, coat pulled on over my chef's jacket while I jiggle my keys in one palm. It's the blessing and curse of owning my own restaurant—I get all the power, all the creativity, but all the responsibilities too.

It never used to bother me, but these days, the long nights chafe a little more than they used to. Because now, I have someone to rush home for. Someone to *miss*, and if I am very lucky and treat her right, someone to miss me.

God, I hope Chloe misses me. Does that make me an asshole? Maybe I don't care. Maybe it's worth the stain on my soul, if she is half as addicted to me as I am to her.

Because I am. Addicted, that is. My fiance is a sugar hit and a caffeine rush and the headiness of the world's finest whiskey, all at once. I begrudge every minute away from her, and on nights when I lock up the restaurant late, I can't help cursing under my breath as I stand on the sidewalk, fiddling with the door.

"Table for two?"

I pause, a slow smile spreading over my cheeks. I don't turn my head, but I don't need to. I'd know that warm, husky voice anywhere.

What is she doing up so late?

"I am afraid we're closed."

There's a hum behind my shoulder. "That's too bad. I hear the food here is the best in the city."

I grunt, spinning the lock again. Opening the restaurant back up. "Depends who you ask, I suppose."

Chloe's chuckle follows me back into the shadowed restaurant. I turn to face her, the door clicking shut and blocking out the late night traffic on the street.

Even shadowed, she's beautiful. The most flawless silhouette: curvy and perfect and *mine*, her dark curls piled high on her head.

Curvier now than before, too. That's partly my unstoppable urge to feed her things, to cook and bake and ice her tiny cupcake treats, and it's partly the small bump already pushing at her belly.

"You shouldn't be awake so late." I'm thinking about that bump, but Chloe scoffs. She's not a woman to be bossed around. And sure enough–

"If you wanted to order me around, Chef Fontaine, you never should have fired me." The words sound harsh, but she's

188

teasing, her voice playful and light.

"Will you ever let me forget that, lovely girl?"

"Of course not." Chloe steps into my open arms, and I tug her close, burying my nose in her hair and breathing in her scent.

I know why she's here, of course. For all her teasing, Chloe misses me on these late nights, too. And when she comes out to the restaurant to meet me, I can never resist pushing her against the wall or kneeling between her legs. But...

"No more late nights," I scold. "Think about our little bump."

Chloe huffs, but to my relief she nods, her hair tickling my nose. And I'm already guiding her to a chair, already nudging her to sit, already kneeling before her, resting my big palms on her knees.

"Thank you for agreeing." She's wearing a soft pair of old leggings. I love her like this—relaxed and carefree—especially since her event planner job is so hectic most days. She thrives in the whirl of it, but I still hate to see her frazzled, so I make it my mission to help her unwind. "I'll make it worth your while."

Chloe hums, scratching gently at my beard. "You're all talk, Chef Fontaine."

I am *not.* And I growl then duck my head, determined to prove it to her.

Ha. My lovely girl plays me like a fiddle.

I don't mind. I'm happy to dance to her tune, especially when it leads me here: eyes closed and tongue sliding over her pussy. She's sweet and salty and warm and wet and *fuck*, I could eat her all night.

"Matthieu." Chloe whispers my name like a prayer. Her fingers card through my hair, holding on tight and tugging, and yes, I know how she feels.

It seems too perfect. Too good to be true.

But it's real, and I'll prove it to her—one night on my knees at a time.

IV

Big Brain

Description

It's the trip of a lifetime–ruined castles and ancient battlefields.

But I can't stop longing for my burly professor.

A year ago, I used to see more of him. Back before the professor's book deal and rise to TV fame, I used to visit his office hours. We'd sit and talk together; going over lecture notes and assignments.

A year ago, it felt like he was *mine.*

He wasn't, obviously. Professor Munro is twice my age–and so off limits it's not even funny. So why do I miss him so badly? Why does my chest ache when we pass in the halls? Why did I sign up for this trip, looking for any excuse to spend a few weeks near him?

And when we finally set foot in Scotland... why does it seem like the professor can't keep away either?

Angie

~⚬✦⚬~

I f someone warned me before I left for college that I'd
fall in love with my professor, here's what I would have
pictured: a slender, dark-haired, serious man, at home
in libraries and bookshops and cramped offices filled with
towering stacks of hardbacks. A man with thick-framed
glasses perched on a patrician nose, and shadows under his
eyes from late nights spent reading.

Tweed jackets and crisp shirts. The scent of stale coffee.

You know the type. A *scholar*.

I'd have pictured the kind of man you walk past on the street
and privately hope that his next meal will have plenty of fruits
and vegetables. A man who doesn't get much sun, and whose
main workout comes from lifting heavy textbooks. The kinds
of professors you see in movies.

I would *not* have expected Professor Munro.

But in my defense—no sane person would. Professor Munro
is inexplicable. He is a law unto himself. That's part of why I
love him.

Picture this: a quiet history department on a rainy college campus. The radiators rattle on the walls; the students' shoes squeak against the floor as they file through the hallways. Everything is *hushed*, and maybe that's the dampening effect of the constant downpour, or maybe it's because everyone inside this building is more concerned with ancient worlds and forgotten wars than the present moment.

There are glass display cases against some of the walls. They contain shards of broken pottery, and trays of wafer-thin metal coins, and polished pieces of bone. When students peer closer to read the descriptions, their breath fogs the smudgy glass.

At the end of the longest hallway, a booming male voice floats through an office door.

Professor Munro runs an open-door policy, welcoming any and all students to drop in to his office for a chat. However, his rumbling baritone carries so easily through wood and thick walls that he keeps the door largely shut out of respect for his neighbors. Despite his best efforts, you can *feel* Professor Munro's words as you approach, vibrating through the floor into the soles of your feet, and you catch snippets of his conversation.

He sounds eager. Quick. Sharply intelligent and brimming with humor, bursting into a loud peal of laughter at something his guest said.

It used to be easy to find time to speak with this man. Back before Professor Munro's book deal and the TV show that made him a minor celebrity, I never had to wait too long for my chance to slip inside his office. He'd offer me a coffee or a glass of orange juice from the mini-fridge rumbling under his desk, and he always, *always*, smiled like he was glad to see me.

Professor Munro remembered my name after the very first

time I met him. Sometimes, when he catches me fidgeting in the front row of lectures, he calls me Antsy Angie, and his eyes always sparkle as he says it.

Even in my first year, when I was so shy I could barely speak, it was different around Professor Munro. Even when I knew barely anything about history, and found the introductory classes worryingly hard, *he* never made me feel anxious like other people did. Professor Munro coaxed me out of my shell, he slipped me chewy toffees from the jar on his desk, he explained the classes without judgment, and he made me feel like...

Well. Like I was somebody. More than plain old Angie Kim.

These days, obviously, there's a constant long line outside his office. Professor Munro is hot shit–TV producers drop by campus to see him. Half the students have crushes on him. Bookshops in big cities try to lure him in to give readings and sign hardbacks of his books. For a while, I tried to keep visiting him too, but it's no use. I can't even get near enough to knock.

Professor Munro doesn't have time for me anymore.

I don't blame him. In my final semester, it's not like I *really* need to speak to him about my assignments–I just like chatting to him. Feeling his keen blue eyes boring into me with rapt interest; hearing his desk chair creak as he leans his big, strong bulk back in it, stroking a hand over his bristly jaw.

I used to like watching the sunlight spill through his office window, glinting in the coppery strands of his brown hair. Some days I had to knot my fingers in my lap to keep from reaching across the desk to pet those dark strands.

Professor Munro has a way of making you feel like the most fascinating person in the whole world. And for a crazy moment there in my second year, I thought maybe he liked *me*. You know, just me. Angie Kim.

Then his TV show took off, and it suddenly all made sense: he's just like that. That's why his fans love him so much—he makes every single person he meets feel special.

So I don't blame him for moving out of my reach. I can watch his TV show and read his books and soak him up that way, the same as everyone else.

It's fine. It's not like he ever *really* saw me anyway.

* * *

I'm on my bed leaning against my headboard, scrolling on my laptop and slurping a giant iced latte through a straw when the email pings into my inbox. It's a Friday night and I'm home alone, my roommates out at a football game I feigned a headache to avoid, so I'm bored enough to sigh and read the email straight away.

You never know. Maybe there's another campus library book swap this weekend.

Chilled coffee rattles through my straw. Rain patters against the dark bedroom window, and I draw a deep mouthful, eyes scanning, lips pursed.

Huh.

I frown. Then scroll back up to the beginning, heart thumping, and check the subject line: *Last minute opportunity!*

It's from him. Professor Munro. Bizarrely, my first thought is: why is he working so late on a Friday night? Is he taking enough breaks? As if he's mine, somehow, to fret over like that. Mine to pester into taking some time off; mine to make sure he's resting that big brain each night.

"Tragic," I mutter, scolding myself, and read the email again, focusing hard on each word. It's written just like Professor Munro speaks–in a boisterous style, larger than life, with each sentence practically leaping off the screen.

Filming a TV episode in Scotland...

Space for two students to help on set...

Handpicked my FAVORITES, of course, so I hope you will both agree to drop everything for my whim...

I grin, nibbling my bottom lip as I reread that line, over and over, double-clicking to highlight it in neon yellow. His favorites, huh? I check the recipients, and yep, there are only two of us. Me, and a quiet guy in the year below called Brian.

Staring at Professor Munro's email signature, I slurp extra hard on my straw then break off coughing, brain freeze ringing in my ears. There's a tiny castle symbol next to his name.

I know before double checking the details that I'll do it–I'll go with Professor Munro to Scotland. Honestly, that man could invite me to a garbage patch and I'd drop everything to go if it meant spending time with him.

Is that pathetic? Maybe. But after this semester, I'll never see him again, so I need to take every chance I get.

The thought of not seeing him anymore makes my chest throb.

But... his favorites. His *favorites.*

I place my half-empty cup on my nightstand, still wheezing.

I crack my knuckles before I type a reply–a horrible habit, and one that my mom always scolds me for. But it feels necessary, somehow. Like I need to gird myself. Like by typing this email, I'm squaring up for battle.

Hi Professor.

His first name is Cameron–a tidbit I discovered years ago

by stalking his college staff profile with its years-out-of-date photo. Just once, I'd like to call him that. *Cameron*. And then I'd like to tease him for that terrible photo. He looks so windblown and rumpled and sexy in it.

Thanks for thinking of me.

Understatement of the century. Knowing that I even crossed Professor Munro's mind—that fact will keep me warm for weeks. Hell, I'll be smug about it on my deathbed.

I'd love to go to Scotland. Of course I'll come.

I type and delete a dozen different sign-offs. They all feel too stiff, too awkward, too revealing. Like I'm letting slip my monster-sized crush in between the lines. In the end, I go with a sign-off that also feels like a confession, but that I can't bring myself to delete once I've written it.

Because it's true. I will always be:

Yours,

Angie Kim

Cameron

I rock back in my office chair and blow out a hard breath, then stare dry-eyed at Angie's reply on my computer screen.

I didn't expect her to write back so quickly–hell, I wasn't sure she'd agree to come at all. It's her last semester, after all, and surely there are hundreds of things that sweet girl would rather do than spend time with an old bastard like me.

God knows I've barely seen her for the last few months–and I've been looking out for her, straining to hear her soft voice in the hall.

But she's coming. It's there in black and white.

Angie's coming to Scotland.

It's the location, I remind myself sternly, tugging open a desk drawer and pulling out a bottle of old scotch and a glass. Seems appropriate. The amber liquid catches the light of my desk lamp as I pour, and I measure out a finger's worth, lecturing myself all the while. *She wants to see Scotland. She's not coming for you.*

No shit. That's why I requested that we make an episode abroad.

I'm not an idiot. I know I don't have much to offer Angie, even if she weren't off-limits as my student. She's beautiful and clever and so adorably serious—a young woman at the beginning of her career. Meanwhile I'm a burly, aging history professor with a loud mouth and a terrible sense of humor. If I want to spend time with her, I need to offer her something better than plain old Professor Munro.

Because sure, I'm having a pinch of success right now. The books are going well; the TV show's popular. But bright, shiny success like that is fleeting, and once it's gone, what will I have left to give her? My dusty old textbooks? Give me a break.

The scotch burns in my throat, spreading smoky warmth through my chest and belly. I stare out of the window at the darkness.

Obviously, the healthy thing would be to leave Angie Kim alone. To let her drift away from me like she's been doing these last few months, and pretend I'm not pining after her like a kicked dog. I should focus on the students who *do* come to see me, and on all the TV meetings and book deadlines that pile up, and stop picturing her there in the empty chair, her long, dark hair slipping out of its braid.

She used to visit all the time. Used to slip inside my office without knocking, like she knew she belonged here, then settle into that chair and fix me with a wry smile. All starchy collars and cute little cardigans. Enamel pins and tiny buttons. Fuck, I wanted her from the first time I saw her.

Sometimes Angie brought questions about her assignments. Sometimes she just wanted to chat about my week–god knows why.

Whatever the reason she had for coming to me, I was always grateful. I always sent up a silent prayer of thanks to any nearby deities listening in, then cracked out my toffee jar and my fanciest instant coffee. And when she left, melting back into the crowded corridor, I always tugged my window shut in a weak attempt to keep her scent in the air.

Because Angie Kim smells like fresh cotton and lemons. Fucking delicious. If they made a candle that smells like her, I'd buy up the whole stock. I'd light one in every room of my house; I'd rub them all over my pillows.

"Crazy bastard," I mutter, swallowing another gulp of scotch. If I heard another professor was obsessing after Angie like this, I'd be pissed off. No, I'd be *livid,* and I'd tell him to watch his fucking step, else he'd have me to answer to.

But who's going to protect Angie Kim from *me*? I slam my glass on the desk, scowling at the email on my screen. I'm such an ass. I did not think this trip through.

…So *I* will. I'll protect her. I'll keep this trip professional, nothing more, and Angie won't ever know how badly I want her. She'll get to see Scotland, and she'll learn about history, and I'll never make her feel uncomfortable–I swear it.

Yeah. It's the only way.

I'll keep my distance from Angie Kim in Scotland if it's the last thing I do.

* * *

"Hi, professor."

I hear those two words all day every day, but when they come in *her* soft voice, they punch me square in the gut. My whole body tenses, and when I turn to face her, I brace myself

203

for the sight of Angie Kim.

She stands on the campus sidewalk, a lilac wheeled suitcase by her side and her black hair tied in two low buns. She's got a thermos of something hot clutched in one hand, and tendrils of steam curl out of the opening, drifting up toward the final stars winking in the early morning sky.

The usually perfect collar of her blouse is flipped up one side. I smooth it down without thinking, then snatch my hand away, heart pounding like I pawed all over her. Jesus. What the hell is wrong with me? My knuckles were so close to her throat then, I could feel her warmth on the air. Flyway strands of her hair tickled my wrist.

"Coffee?" Desperate to distract us both, I nod at the thermos in her hand.

Angie's mouth twists in a smile. "You know it."

I *do* know it. This girl has a serious coffee addiction, and sometimes when she drinks too many before lectures, she gets so twitchy I call her Antsy Angie. I'd have bet my life savings on those wisps of steam being coffee-scented.

"On you get, then." I jerk my chin at the college minibus idling by the sidewalk. Its engine rumbles steadily as it warms up, the only sound on campus this early in the morning. "Scotland waits for no woman."

Angie snorts, dragging her suitcase past me to the back of the minibus.

Brian's already here—a tall, gawky third year with messy fair hair. He's buckled into a seat, a travel guide to Scotland held a few inches from his narrow face, and he squints as he reads in the dim morning light. I should be glad he was punctual, but mostly I'm mourning the stolen moments alone I could have had with Angie.

No.

That's not what this trip is about. It's about filming a TV episode, and giving these two something great for their resumes. It's not about–not about *that.* My shameful crush on a much younger student. Fuck.

"Seat belts on." After stowing Angie's suitcase, I swing myself into the driver's seat and slam the door closed. This is what I'll do: I'll take refuge in responsibilities. Keeping everything safe and efficient; making sure this trip goes off without a hitch. "It's a two hour drive to the airport. Radio on or off?"

"Off," Brian calls.

Angie shrugs in the rear-view mirror, her brown eyes burning into mine.

I clear my throat, mouth suddenly dry. Off it is.

The minibus rocks as we pull away from the sidewalk, the red brick campus buildings slipping past on either side. It's still cold out, condensation misting the windscreen, but the first fragile blossoms clinging to the bare trees mark the arrival of spring. I focus on driving, on the swaying bulk of the minibus, and I try to ignore the pretty, pale face watching me in the rear view mirror.

Angie shouldn't stare at me like that. Nor at *any* man. With the intense frown puckering her forehead, she looks almost hungry–like she's as starved for the sight of me these days as I am for her.

A man might get ideas, when a young woman looks at him like that. Wrong ideas. Ideas he has no business having.

I curse under my breath, shaking my head as I pull us off campus onto the highway.

This was a terrible idea.

Angie

❧◦✦◦❧

Professor Munro looks at home in a castle. He's got that *look* about him: that rugged, windswept vibe that makes you think of roaring fires in great halls and thick tapestries hung on stone walls. He's *wild*. Untamed. A creature of the landscape, with a thick beard I want to plunge my fingers into and auburn streaks in his brown hair.

Even dressed in dark jeans and a flannel shirt, his big body looks like it belongs on ancient battlefields. Like he should be swinging an ax or a great sword, his cheeks ruddy and his blue eyes fierce. *Damn.*

I see why his TV show is so popular. Even if I didn't care at all about history, I'd tune in to watch this man prowling through ruined halls. No wonder so many students have crushes on him now. No wonder I can't get close to him even when I try.

"Cut!"

The producer's sharp voice echoes around the stone hall, and I jolt back to the present, fumbling my clipboard. I'm supposed to be watching Professor Munro, I really am, but I should be checking for inconsistencies between takes. Things in the background out of place–that kind of thing.

Not staring at my professor with so much longing it makes my chest ache.

Did he notice? God, I hope not. How humiliating.

As the TV crew bustle around, moving the cameras and kicking thick black cables out of the way, I duck my head and scribble notes on my clipboard. Anything to avoid Professor Munro's clever gaze. He's chatting with the assistant director, his back to a roaring fire in the stone hearth, and the pops and crackles of the fire fill the gaps in their murmured conversation. But even as he talks to the other man, his eyes keep drifting to me.

I shift my feet, my toes cold inside my sneakers. How did anyone ever keep warm inside this castle? It's so freezing, it's like the chill seeps directly through the stone floor.

"Okay, Angie?"

I'm ready when Professor Munro comes over to me. I see him coming; I have a few vital seconds to prepare. So I manage to nod and smile like a normal human being, and I even flip around my clipboard to show him my notes.

"Yep. It's really cool being on set. Thanks again for bringing us."

Across the room, Brian's chatting with a camera man, nodding and listening with folded arms. We're all bundled up in sweaters and jeans against the cold, the collar of my pale blue shirt smoothed carefully on top of my black sweater. It may be springtime, but it's still Scotland. It's freaking freezing.

Professor Munro smiled when he saw my outfit this morning–my Peter Pan collar and the strawberry enamel pin on my sweater. It was like he was sharing a joke with himself, but not in a mean way.

I flushed hot all over when I saw that smile, and my cheeks haven't stopped burning since. God, he makes me feel so *seen*.

"You're welcome." When Professor Munro smiles, his eyes crinkle, and his forehead smooths out. I love watching it—his face is so mobile. So expressive. Every thought, every emotion, gets broadcast there for all to see.

Right now, the professor is happy and a little bored. The filming is dragging on, and he's not a man for standing still.

"Don't worry. I heard the producer say we'll be done soon."

His smile stretches wider. "That obvious, am I, Angie?"

I shrug. "To me, you are."

He blinks, and my heart drops as I play back my own words. It's—I'm *flirting*, there's no other word for it, and it's so freaking obvious and clumsy that I want to melt into the floor.

I swallow hard, staring past Professor Munro at the fire leaping in the hearth.

He rescues me from myself. Of course he does. He's like one of those old knights—noble and kind.

"Do you have any questions about the castle?"

I do. Thank god. Even if I didn't, I'd make some up just to keep him talking to me. And so we kill fifteen minutes together, talking about history and kings and siege tactics while the camera crew ready their equipment. When he catches me shivering, Professor Munro takes my elbow and gently tugs me closer to the fire.

"I still don't really know why I'm here," he tells me quietly once I've run out of questions. He waves a big hand up and down his body. "There must be some young history hotshot that would bring them more viewers."

His tone is jovial, but I snort. I can't help it. "Hardly." My cheeks flush warm under his piercing gaze, but I make myself say it. This man deserves to know how wonderful he is. "I can't think of anyone better. There's no one I'd rather watch on TV, or read books by. You're…" I squeeze my clipboard as I search for the perfect words. My paper crinkles in my grip. "You're magic. Everything they think and more."

It's too much.

God, I've said so much, and every part of me is screaming that I need to get out of here, need to go sprinting across the rolling grassy hills outside and scream up at the puffy white clouds, and maybe throw myself into the moat for good measure. But Professor Munro stares at me with something like awe on his face, and when he beams, it's the first time all day that I've been warm down to my bones.

"Ah, Angie. You're a good girl. Far too sweet to an old bastard like me."

"You're not *old*," I say hotly, so annoyed that I forget to keep my voice down. He's insulting the object of my affection, after all. We should *both* be offended. "You're just… you're seasoned."

Professor Munro tips his head back and roars with laughter, the sound bouncing off the ceiling. All around, crew members glance over, and across the room, Brian's eyebrows climb his forehead.

Whatever. I shuffle a few inches away, hot and flustered. It's *true*. Professor Munro is not old. He's a vintage whiskey, a fine wine, and any girl would be lucky to have him.

"Thirty seconds," the assistant director calls, watching me with an odd expression.

I stumble away from the fire, the chill seeping back through my clothes the further across the room I go. My sneakers slap against the dusty flagstones, and I pick my way over cables and between silver and black equipment cases.

My grip is sweaty on my pen as I spin around and prepare to take more notes.

I don't know why they're all staring at me like that. There's nothing to see here.

***

Two hours later, I lean against a ruined castle wall and watch the sun sink toward the horizon. It's fiery red, the thick bank of clouds lit crimson from below, and in every direction there's nothing but grassy hills and marshy shrubland.

A cold breeze tugs at my ponytail, and I burrow deeper into my jacket as I wait. Heavy footsteps crunch against the loose stones behind me, but I already know it's him without turning around.

I *always* know when it's Professor Munro. It's like I'm tuned into him, my senses hyper-aware to his movements.

"Red sky at night…" His voice is rough after speaking all day for the cameras. He waits, and I finish the saying gamely, still not turning away from the sunset.

"…Shepherd's delight. Hey, professor."

"Hi, Angie."

More footsteps crunch against the path, and then he comes to stand behind me. Not touching, but still close enough that his bulk blocks most of the wind, his warmth washing over me instead.

I bite my lip, staring harder at the horizon.

"It's good seeing you." Professor Munro's words come slower than usual. Like he's picking his words carefully. "You don't come by my office so much anymore."

Sudden tears burn in my eyes, and I blink them away hard, my breaths coming short. It's so ridiculous. He's my professor and he's making polite conversation—he doesn't know about the pit of loneliness that yawns open in my stomach whenever I think about *him*. Whenever I think about how much time we used to have together, before... well. Before.

I clear my throat, but my words still sound hoarse. "You're a busy man, professor."

"I still want to see you, Angie. I always want to see you."

Warmth spreads through my stomach, but I try to ignore it. I lift one shoulder. "Even so. You're a hard man to get hold of these days. And I get it," I add quickly, in case Professor Munro thinks I'm complaining. I'm *glad* he's so successful—he deserves everything he has and more. "It's not like I have questions about my classes when I can't see you. I don't have real problems to bring you or anything, so it's right that other people get you first."

Professor Munro grumbles something under his breath. He sounds surprisingly bitter for such a jovial man.

Then: "I don't just want your problems, Angie. I want all of it."

I fold my arms tighter across my chest, like I can keep my racing heart from bursting out of my ribs. "Even the boring stuff? Like hearing about my day?"

And god, what professor wants that from his student? It's so pathetic, and I don't dare to turn around. But when Professor Munro rumbles "Especially that," I melt against the stone wall, weak with relief.

His footsteps crunch against the path as he walks away. Cold air washes over my back and I screw my eyes shut, missing him already, listening to his booming voice drift across the grounds as he calls to the crew.

He thinks I don't want his company anymore?

For a smart man, he has no freaking idea.

Cameron

It's nine PM in a pub in Scotland, and I can't stop staring at my student. The TV crew picked this place for us to stay a few nights, and they chose well–the building feels almost as old as the hills, with its dark wood beams and the scent of wood smoke hanging in the air. A fire crackles in a stone fireplace, and dozens of iron pokers hang on the walls.

Locals cluster around the bar and slump in booths together, swigging from foamy dark ales and bursting into laughter.

Angie sits across from me in our booth, her hands wrapped around a dark ale of her own. I raised my eyebrows when she ordered it, but she primly told me that she's plenty old enough to drink, thank-you-very-much, and *fuck.* I love when she gets on her high horse.

Brian is next to Angie, and I am trying hard not to be a jealous asshole about that. Unlike my girl, Brian is *not* old enough to drink, at least not back home, so he's nursing a soda and feeling sorry for himself.

When he catches me grinning at his soda, Brian huffs and

shakes his head, but his lips twitch. Yeah, he's not really mad. He's a good kid.

They both are. Fuck, I need to leave her alone.

A few members of the TV crew take up the rest of the booth, cramming us in tight until we're elbow-to-elbow. There's a constant stream of people wandering up to the bar and coming back; an endless circulation of full and empty glasses. We shuffle around the booth, letting one person out then making space for another, and damn, these TV people can really drink.

Angie's noticed too. Her cheeks are flushed, her eyes extra-bright, but she's still nursing her first ale, her grip flexing against the glass. And when the assistant director squeezes into the booth, his movements sloppy, Angie shoots me a conspiratorial grin.

I wink back at her.

Her cheeks flush darker.

Next to Angie, Brian's eyebrows twitch, but when I pin him with a look, his narrow face is blank. He pointedly looks away, staring out of the booth.

Good. Fine. There's nothing for him to see here, anyway. I'm not doing anything wrong by glancing at Angie now and then, and sending her a quick wink–that doesn't *mean* anything.

It's not like I'm doing what I *want* to be doing. I'm not shoving my way around the booth until Angie's slender body is pressed up against my side; I'm not dragging her onto my lap and jiggling her on my thighs until she bursts out in bright laughter.

I'm not sliding my fingers through her soft, black hair.

Not tilting her head back and covering her mouth with mine.

And I'm not sweeping every glass off the table onto the floor, then spreading Angie Kim out on the wood like my personal feast, right here for every asshole to see me stake my claim.

So, yeah. I'm being very fucking restrained. Brian can wipe that knowing look off his face any time he likes.

"Stone circle tomorrow." The producer's voice is thick. Fuzzy with drink. He leans forward, long blond hair tied back in a knot, and pins us all with a glare. "We're leaving at dawn. Taking the ferry over. You sleep in, you get left behind."

When he reaches Angie, his stare lingers a beat too long and she stiffens, grip going still on her glass. I bristle, but then he's moved on, talking to a crew member further along.

He'd better not look at her like that again. I don't care if he's writing my paycheck–*no one* makes Angie Kim uncomfortable. Not while I'm around.

Brian catches my eye again and I glower out at the pokers above the fireplace, trying not to feel like the world's worst hypocrite.

* * *

I time my exit perfectly with Angie's. Not for any creepy reason, but because this is a goddamn pub full of boozed-up men, and I want to make sure she gets back to her room okay. I don't trust these fuckers. Not with someone so precious.

Angie delivers her empty glass back to the bar as she leaves, muttering a soft thanks to the barman. I trail after her, glowering whenever it looks like a drinker might get in her way, and grunting when they do the smart thing and move.

I'm a caveman. She's sent me back in time. I'm a heartbeat away from tossing her over my shoulder and sprinting out into the darkness, hollering that she's mine.

I don't, though. And I know I shouldn't get brownie points for being a decent human being, but it *feels* like I need some kind of medal for keeping my greedy hands off her as we climb the flight of narrow, wooden stairs.

"Did you like your ale?"

I fix my eyes on the back of her hair, refusing to let my eyes drop lower, but even the sight of her silky black ponytail swinging back and forth with each step is enough to make me bite back a groan.

"Sure." Angie glances back at me, and even though she's further up the steps, I'm still taller. "I drank it all, didn't I? Honestly, when I bought it I kind of thought it would be gross, but it turns out I liked it."

"You're an adventurous girl, Angie Kim."

She snorts, turning away as she climbs higher. "If you say so, professor."

I do. I *do* say so. She came all this way, didn't she? She crossed an ocean at short notice to be here. And she's been great on set over the last week–such a quick learner, always happy to muck in and do what needs to be done, and I'm pretty sure that half the men in the crew already want to keep her.

"I'm glad you're here, Angie." Mad bursts of jealousy aside. "I'll miss you when you graduate."

She sucks in a sharp breath, her steps slowing as she climbs. And once we spill out of the stairwell, walking along a dim corridor, Angie doesn't say anything. She strides in front of me, thoughtful and quiet.

I deliver her right to her door. That's why I'm here, right? To keep her safe. To make sure she gets back okay. I even get her to unlock it, poking my head through the doorway to make sure everything's really fine before I go.

There's a squashy single bed against one wall, piled high with a patchwork bedspread, and a nightstand with a fringed table lamp. Angie's lilac suitcase stands in one corner, and the outfit she's picked out for tomorrow already hangs against the closet door, the creases dropping out before she puts it on in the morning.

The sight of that pretty cream blouse and green cardigan–it makes my heart lurch. She's so neat and delicate and perfect. Everything I'm not.

"Okay." I back into the corridor, mind reeling. "It all looks good. Knock on my door if you need anything, sweetheart."

Sweetheart. Shit. I shouldn't call her that–not even in my head, and definitely not out loud. But it's out there now, hanging between us in the air, and I can't take it back even if I want to.

I'm not sure I want to.

Especially when Angie blinks up at me, lips parting in surprise. My pulse hammers in my throat as my student studies me, dark eyes considering. And as I watch, she seems to make some kind of decision.

Then she rocks up onto her toes, one hand braced against my shoulder, and brushes her lips against my cheek. It's barely a whisper of a touch, but fuck–my heart slams hard enough to crack a rib.

I wait, frozen, until she settles back onto her heels. The sounds of the pub seep through the floor, mingling with our breaths.

Surely she can hear my heartbeat, too. It's *deafening.*

"Goodnight, Professor Munro."

For once in my life, I can't speak. I nod at her, watching dumbstruck as Angie steps into her room and shyly closes the door behind her. Once I'm safely alone, I brush my cheek with my fingertips, the spot where she kissed me still tingling madly under my beard.

It meant nothing.

Or at least, I know she meant nothing by it.

But as I turn at last and drift to my own room, I'll be damned if that tiny kiss didn't mean everything to *me*.

Angie

The stone circle stands on a hill, the pale sky yawning wide overhead. It's exposed out here, nothing but low-lying heather and gorse all around, and when I spin around, I can see clumps of white stone buildings, a patchwork of fields, and the distant ocean frothing against the shore.

The standing stones are *huge.* They lurch out of the landscape like crooked teeth, and as the crew mill around and we get ready to film, it's like the stones are watching us. Silent and all-knowing. The hairs prickle on the back of my neck, and when I glance over at Brian by the van, he looks unsettled too.

"Spooky," Brian mutters, glancing at me.

I duck my chin, smiling down at my clipboard. Out of the corner of my eye, Professor Munro's flannel shirt flaps in the strong breeze as he approaches. He's another miracle of nature–completely impervious to the cold. I bet he could swim in icy rivers and lakes without even uttering a peep.

"Definitely. They make me think of ancient sacrifices, or something."

Professor Munro hums as he comes to stand next to us, his voice warm with approval. "Very primal of you, Angie."

I scoff, tapping my pen against my paper, but I can't think what else to say. Ever since last night, I've been replaying that stolen moment together over and over.

Professor Munro calling me *sweetheart* in that gruff, low voice.

The empty corridor, filled only with our breaths.

The softness of his beard beneath my lips.

I don't know why, but I thought his beard would be wirier. Kind of scratchy. But it wasn't, not at all, and now I can't stop thinking about rubbing my cheek against his face, purring and butting up against him like a cat.

"Sleep well?" His voice is rough, and when I risk a glance over, he looks tired. Wan, with shadows under his blue eyes, but happy too. And I find my nerves easing, the mad fluttering of my pulse slowing down as I smile back, suddenly feeling as rooted and steady as the stones.

"Nope. I didn't."

Those keen eyes are knowing. "Oh? Did something keep you awake, Angie Kim?"

I lick my lips, hardly believing my own daring. But I do–I say it, gripping tight to my clipboard for safety. Glancing at Brian to make sure he's not listening. "Something. Or someone."

Professor Munro's chest expands, and it's like we're the only two here. The only people for miles around as he heaves another breath and I stare at him, not willing to even blink in case I shatter the moment.

He *wants* me. I know he does. I never dreamed that he could, but since arriving in Scotland, things have been different. Undeniable.

And I sure as hell want him. More than I've ever wanted anything in my entire life. Even just standing here like this, not touching and barely speaking–it's lighting me up from the inside. Bathing my insides with warm, golden light, and god, I wish we weren't here to film. I wish we could run off, just the two of us. I wish he could press me against one of these stones, and… and…

"One minute," a crew member calls, and we jerk back to reality. Professor Munro turns away, ruddy face flushing above his beard, and I clear my throat, throwing another glance at Brian.

The other student nods at me, his fair hair ruffled by the breeze. His gaze is knowing, and my spine stiffens automatically in response.

"We were just talking about the stones."

"I didn't say anything," Brian says mildly, and my stomach squirms as I watch filming begin.

Are we that obvious?

Will the TV company care?

Could I get Professor Munro in trouble over this?

I'm not stupid. *I* know that what we have isn't seedy–that it's based on more than physical attraction. Honestly, sometimes the time I spend with Professor Munro feels like the purest thing in my life.

But I know how it must look, too: an older man, a professor with power over his student, and a handpicked opportunity abroad.

The notes on my paper blur as I stare blindly at my clipboard, the edges flapping in the wind.

I should be stronger, for both our sakes. I should stay away from Professor Munro.

* * *

Deciding to keep away from Professor Munro and actually doing it are two different things. For one, it's hard to avoid the star of a TV show when you're helping on set. For another, every hour of this trip is accounted for by our tight schedule, from the time spent crammed in the hired vans together to the nights in crowded, smoky inns. I can't slip away. Can't head off for a day on my own. For another week, my schedule is entwined with his.

Even less helpful to my mission is the fact that Professor Munro is really protective. He doesn't like leaving me or Brian alone for too long with the crew, and he hovers over us when we stop in pubs for the night until we both go to our rooms. I'd worry about how obvious he's being, except that he's super protective of Brian, too.

A small, ugly part of me is kind of bitter about that. I know it's terrible, but I wouldn't hate if *all* of his focus was on me.

Who am I kidding? I'd freaking love it. I want to take a warm bath in Professor Munro's undivided attention.

"Angie Kim."

I press my lips together, fighting a smile as I wait at the bar in our inn for the night. All around me is a wall of dark jackets, and I could be here for hours trying to catch the bartender's eye.

Despite that, I'm in a good mood. I love when Professor Munro says my whole name like that–like he's relishing it. Like it tastes delicious in his mouth.

"Yes, professor?"

He squeezes through the crowd, coming to stand next to my elbow. "I have something to show you. Want to see a famous Scottish beastie?"

I lose my battle against the smile. "Obviously," I murmur, and my heart stutters as he takes my arm, drawing me out of the crowd.

The heat of the pub fades away as we near the back door, propped open against the cold, velvety darkness. Our breaths form little white puffs in front of our chins, and as we cross the parking lot, Professor Munro's grip slides down my arm until our fingers tangle together, his bigger hand dwarfing mine.

Holy crap. This is happening.

I swallow hard. The stars pulse and glitter overhead.

"You could get in trouble," I tell him quietly, voice hoarse. "You shouldn't risk it. Someone might see."

I don't let go, though, and Professor Munro squeezes my fingers in response, his strides slowing to match mine.

"You're probably right, sweetheart. But it's dark enough out here to be brave, don't you think?"

I'm almost surprised when he leads me to a wooden fence with scraggly grass clumped around its posts. As though the Scottish beastie thing was all a lie. But no—Professor Munro points through the gloom, his clothes rustling in the quiet, and it takes a second for my eyes to adjust before I see it.

A cow. A Highland cow, with long brown fur and gleaming white horns, just like we've seen on tourist posters and embroidered on dish towels.

"Huh." The cow's head swings around slowly, staring back at us through the shadows.

"Cool, right?"

"Definitely." God, his hand is so warm. He's like a radiator on legs. "Don't laugh, but I kind of wondered if these were a myth."

Professor Munro's snort is loud. It echoes across the silent field.

"*Angie*. It's a cow, not the Loch Ness monster."

"Well, I'd never seen one! And we've been here for a week already."

His thumb rubs over the back of my hand, scorching a gentle trail. "So we have. It's been a good first week."

It really has. Out here... it's like we've fallen off the map. The real world, with classes and graduation and job applications and consequences—it all feels a thousand miles away.

"I don't want to go back."

He grunts in agreement. "Maybe we'll stay here, then. Grow old together in this field."

It's my turn to laugh, though it comes out strangled. I know he's joking, but I can think of far worse things.

Things like never seeing him again.

Things like going back to campus and constantly missing him, knowing he's nearby but never getting past the line outside his office.

And thinking about those things... my chest gets tight. It's like there's a bubble growing inside my ribs, squeezing my heart and my lungs and making everything ache, getting bigger and bigger and tighter until I can't *stand* it any more.

I spin around and throw my arms around Professor Munro's neck.

He catches me with an *oof*, gathering me against his chest like it's the most natural thing in the world. And I meant to just hug him, I swear, but as soon as his breath mists hot against my cheek, I *need* him.

I choke back a sob.

And kiss the professor hard.

It's rough–like I want to bruise him. Like I want to leave a mark. And I didn't know I had it in me, didn't know I had *any* of this in me, but it's definitely me, it's Angie Kim nipping her professor's bottom lip. It's Angie Kim parting her lips for him and deepening the kiss; it's Angie Kim sucking on his tongue.

And it's Professor Munro, groaning like a broken man. It's him flattening his palms against my back and pressing me hard against his body, close enough to feel his heart thumping under his flannel shirt.

He tastes like ale. Like the apple he ate in the van. His beard tickles my cheeks.

God, I want to scramble up him and never get down again.

"Ah, fuck." We're both breathing hard when we break away, puffing out clouds of frozen air. "Angie. Fuck. I shouldn't have done that."

"You didn't do it. *I* did."

Professor Munro chuckles, and I press closer again. If he wants to be rid of me, he'll have to peel me off like a bandaid.

"I took your hand," he says reasonably, his words warm against my cheek. "I brought you out here all alone."

"And I kissed you. If you'll stop arguing, professor, I'll kiss you again."

We're silent for a long time after that. There's only the rustle of our clothes and the scrape of our boots against the loose stones, and the occasional stifled moan or soft curse.

I can't keep him. I do know that.

But we stay outside for a little while longer anyway, clinging together under the stars.

Cameron

I can't sleep.

How am I supposed to ever sleep again when Angie Kim kissed me like that? Throwing her whole heart and soul into the task, moaning into my mouth like she was just as wrecked by it as I was? Clinging to me like she needed safety from a storm?

Fuck. There'll be no recovering from this. I can't unfeel it. Can't forget the way she tasted. My blood's still pumping fast through my veins; my skull's pounding with the need to go and find her, to snatch her into my arms again.

I'm ruined. That young woman has ruined me.

Jesus. This is bad.

I'm a zombie all through the hurried breakfast with the crew, barely speaking to anyone and downing coffee after coffee, trying to blink away the exhaustion of a sleepless night. Though I tell myself not to look at her, a glance down the table shows Angie isn't much better than me this morning–her red sweater looks more rumpled than usual, and her silky black

227

hair is slipping out of uneven bunches.

I *feel* it every time she looks over this way, but I don't look back. I don't trust myself not to give everything away, staring at her moon-eyed down the length of the table.

Two hours later, we're filming in a grand hunting lodge on the edge of a loch. It's an old building, filled with famous oil paintings and priceless tapestries and the bearskin rugs on chilly flagstones. Angie wrinkles her nose in disapproval when she sees the rugs, and I choke back a laugh as the crew order me into place in front of another lit hearth.

Yeah, I didn't think she'd like that. It's history, though—albeit a brutal part of it.

The makeup artist tuts over the bags under my eyes, and despite her heroic attempts at covering me up, I can tell from her grumbling that I look like shit as the camera rolls. I still do my best, working through the script and trying to muster some desperate dregs of energy, but it doesn't come easily like it normally does.

It's *work*. Even with the steady stream of coffees in takeout cups; even with the ruthless efficiency of the crew. And for once in my life, I'd like nothing more than to call it quits—to admit defeat and slink back to the van and catch a few hours of sleep in the passenger seat. But the crew are relying on me, and Angie Kim is watching, and she looks so *sure* of me as she grips her clipboard, her lips curled in a soft smile. Like I can do no wrong in her eyes. Like I'm her hero.

It's a heady feeling, that. No—it's fucking *addictive*.

I want it every day for the rest of my life. I want to make *her* feel this way, like she's a hundred feet tall, and I want to march over there and take that clipboard off her, want to toss it at Brian and sweep Angie into my arms.

"Cameron?" I jolt, turning to the producer. He's watching me closely, arms folded over his chest. "Ready to go again?"

"Sure." My throat is tight when I swallow. "I'm ready. Yes."

Because I can't do any of that. Angie Kim is not mine, no matter how badly I want her, no matter that we kissed.

It's just the romance of Scotland, getting to her head and making her smile at me like that—not me.

* * *

I'm pacing my room after midnight when there's a soft knock on the door. We're in another old-fashioned pub with dark wood beams on the ceilings and cramped guest rooms, and there's barely space for me to prowl up and down between the lumpy double bed and the wall.

I freeze, heart pounding.

No one else would come to my room this late, never mind that the pub's still serving drinks, the din floating up through the floor. If one of the crew wanted me, they'd text or call, and if they *did* knock, it'd be a solid thump against the wood. Not that shy little tap.

My voice is hoarse. "Come in, Angie."

She slips through the doorway like a shadow, still dressed in her red sweater and jeans. Her cute little sneakers squeak against the floorboards, far dirtier than they were one week ago.

"Hi, professor." The door clicks shut in the frame. Angie leans against it, palms pressed against the wood, and her smile is so nervous it breaks my heart. "Is it okay that I'm here?"

Always.

I splutter a laugh. "Not really, no. But don't go," I add quickly when she slumps and reaches for the handle. Fuck, I am a weak man when it comes to her. But she's hovering, unsure, and I hate that, hate how wrong it feels, so I rake a hand through my messy hair, searching for the words to wipe those nerves off her face.

"I've been telling myself all day I'll be a better man, Angie. That I'll leave you alone and not take advantage, not even if by some miracle you come to me again. But now you're here, sweetheart, and I didn't sleep last night for thinking of you, and I've fucking wanted you all day, and you're making a liar of me, Angie Kim."

As I talk, she pushes off the door, crossing the small room with a determined glint in her eyes. And my arms are already open wide when she reaches me; I'm already ducking my head. I can't fight it, no matter how awful it makes me.

I want her.

Right at this moment, I'd rather die than keep away.

"You wouldn't look at me today," Angie murmurs between kisses. My neck twinges from bending down to reach her, and screw it, I grab her ass and lift her. Hold her with her legs wrapped around my waist, plastered to my front, exactly as she should be.

"I didn't trust myself."

"No?" She tightens her arms around my neck, mouthing at my jaw. "Why not, professor?"

That teasing lilt to her voice—the roll of her hips against mine—*fuck*. Angie Kim is a bombshell. She's shaving off years of my life.

"You know why." The words come out harsh, guttural, but Angie only smirks against my cheek, squirming closer. I palm her ass through her jeans before giving her a quick smack, and it's my turn to grin when her breath catches. "If I looked at you, I wouldn't have made it through the damn day, sweetheart. Not without tossing you over my shoulder in front of everyone and carrying you off like a caveman. Not without pressing you against one of those frayed old tapestries and making you moan so loud it echoed through the halls."

There's a stifled whimper, then sharp teeth nip my earlobe. Jesus Christ. And everything's hazy, drowned out by the fever crackling through my body and the *thump-thump-thump* of my racing heart as I turn and toss Angie onto the center of my mattress.

She bounces, spluttering and red-cheeked, limbs flying everywhere as the bed springs wail.

I grin at her, one knee already on the bed.

Fuck keeping my distance. Fuck restraint. Angie Kim came to me tonight. She's *mine*. And she knows that, she sees that, because she spreads her legs for me as naturally as breathing, making space for me to crawl on top.

I duck my head, licking a stripe up her throat.

"*God.*" Angie claws at my shirt, tugging at the fabric like she's forgotten how buttons work. I love that. She can tear it if she wants. She can do anything she damn well likes. "This is—I didn't think it would be like this. It's—it's so—"

I lift my head, peering down at her. My girl's flushed and crumpled. She's bright-eyed and dazed with wet, shining lips, and it takes every ounce of my self control not to lower my bulk and flatten her, rutting her into the mattress.

"Feeling overwhelmed, sweetheart?"

Because I *can* stop, obviously. I'm not an animal. But I'll admit I'm almost lightheaded with relief when Angie shakes her head. I balance on one elbow, reaching between us to brush a stray strand of hair off the corner of her mouth.

"You want to keep going?"

A nod this time. "Yes. Definitely. But I–I don't really know what I'm doing. Um. With this." She waves between us, her knuckles brushing my chest, and for a professor, it takes me way too long to realize what she's saying. Then–

"Ah, fuck." I can't help it. I lower down another inch, plastering my big body over her slender one. Feeling her every angle and curve. And maybe I should be embarrassed about the soft press of my stomach, but when Angie inhales sharply and rolls her body up against mine, I can't think of anything except feeling more of her.

"Your first time doing this kind of thing, huh?" The tip of my nose trails over her throat, her cheek, her chin, and I inhale the whole way. Fresh cotton and lemons. "That's a hell of a gift, Angie. You sure you want to give it to me?"

She yanks harder on my shirt in answer. "Please, professor."

"Cameron," I grit out. My hips press down against her, thrusting her rhythmically against the bed. "My name is Cameron."

Angie giggles, and she sounds lightheaded too. "I know. I looked up at your staff profile online. That *photo*."

Ha, oh god. I forgot about that old photo. I look insane in it. Like a viking someone wrestled into a suit. But the fact that she found it, that she cared enough to look me up, means I can't bring myself to be embarrassed.

I'll pretend, though. For dignity's sake.

"That's it." My grin is savage as I shove upright, scrabbling at her jeans button. Still giggling, Angie lifts her hips to help me work them down her thighs. "I'll teach you to mock your professor, Angie Kim."

Her laughter cuts off abruptly, melting into a groan as I rub the pad of my thumb over the fabric of her panties. She's hot and damp, scorching through the thin cotton, and that *wet* patch...

That fucking wet patch.

"I'm going to taste you." I sound more like a beast than a man, the words growling out of me as I shoulder my way between her thighs. "Say you'll let me, Angie. Say you'll let me lick you. I'll teach you to laugh at an old man. Jesus Christ."

She laughs, and she sounds winded, propping herself up on her elbows to watch as she says, "I'll let you. Prof–Cameron. I'll *obviously* let you."

Obviously.

That one word means the world to me. Like this feels as inevitable to her as it does to me. Like I haven't been alone in this for months, for *years,* pining after this girl when all I wanted to do was–well. This.

I bend my head, mouthing at the hot, damp cotton. Angie moans, already bucking her hips up to meet my mouth, and *yes,* I've got a wildcat on my hands. I flatten a palm over her stomach, pinning her down to the bed, and for the next few minutes I set about showing her just how badly I've wanted her all this time.

Pressing messy, open mouthed kisses to her mound, I make her breath catch.

I make her squirm.

I make her buck.

I make her whimper and moan and *beg* me for more, and only then do I tug her panties to the side, sliding my hot tongue through her swollen flesh. That slickness is more proof, further evidence that she wants me too, and I rumble out a desperate groan as I lick it up, tasting her on my tongue.

Angie Kim is wet for me.

This is a hell of a day.

"Your beard tickles."

I huff a laugh, rubbing my cheeks against her trembling thighs as I lick her, suck her, nibble gently at her clit. And those thighs clamp tighter around my head, holding me in place like there's a risk I'll stop what I've started.

No chance.

I won't take all her firsts. Not tonight. But Angie Kim is going to come on my tongue if it's the last thing I do.

There's no more time for words. No room for anything except working her over, my breaths panting ragged against her core, her thighs squeezing my ears and muffling all sounds except the thrum of my pulse. Angie twitches with every lick, her ass squeezed in my palms, and when her stomach tenses, her legs locking tight, it's the closest thing to a religious experience I've ever had.

She comes on my tongue, so perfect and shameless. With such a pretty gasp.

Mine. My Angie.

When I finally sit up, my jaw's aching like the devil and my beard's slick with what we've done. Angie lies limp on my bed, but when I lean down to kiss her, she returns it hungrily.

She wriggles her jeans up her hips, then we talk for a while. Lie close but not touching, murmuring quietly about nothing at all. And when Angie yawns so hard her jaw cracks, I know what's coming. Know it, and hate it already.

"You could stay," I offer, but she's shaking her head. I know she's right, but my heart sinks anyway.

What did I think would happen? That she'd borrow one of

my shirts to sleep in? That she'd let me spoon her, holding her tight against me through the night?

"No, I'd better not." Angie rolls over with a groan and swings her legs to the floor, like *she's* the one who did all the work. Cheeky minx. "We shouldn't risk it. I don't want to get you in trouble."

I scoff, but my gut churns at her words. She's worried about *me?* I'm not the only one at risk here, but I'm definitely the one doing wrong, and shame washes over me, hot and queasy, at the thought.

"You're right," I rasp. "Better not risk it." My chest is tight as I walk her to the door and kiss her forehead. "Goodnight, sweetheart."

Angie slips out into the corridor, cheeks flushed and eyes bright, and I watch her go with a lump of dread in my belly.

Angie

❦

I sneak into Cameron's room for every night left of the trip. Five stolen nights together. Five different lumpy beds, covered with fraying patchwork bedspreads. The professor answers my knock every night without complaint, a mixture of relief and hunger etched on his handsome face, and though he kisses me *everywhere* until I'm squirming for relief, he never lets us go any further.

He never lets me repay the favor either, ridiculous man. Can it be so hard to believe that I *want* to put my mouth on him?

Despite my mounting frustration for more, the nights are perfect. Flushed pockets of paradise, carved out together in the Scottish countryside. In the daytime, though, everything is different. It has to be.

So we keep our distance.

We barely look at each other.

We keep it *professional*, even bordering on cold.

Brian asks me about it one morning, checking everything is okay. I shrug and nod, helping to unwind a thick TV cable, and Brian lets it drop but he doesn't look convinced.

And I get it. After every extra night together, after every estranged day, we're getting closer and closer to going home. Back to reality; back to the unreachable professor. Back to 'off-limits' and nights alone in my student bedroom.

Of course I'm not okay. I don't want this to end.

On our last night in Scotland, Professor Munro takes a long time to answer my knock. I wait in the inn hallway, head spinning and stomach twisting, my forehead tipped forward to rest against the wooden door.

Please.

I know it has to end. I *do*. But we have one more night together, don't we?

"Angie. Come in, sweetheart." His door swings open eventually, and Cameron smiles at me like he never hesitated at all. He pushes the door wide and I duck under his arm, and the familiar scent of his body as I pass makes my chest pinch.

Fresh air and soft flannel. Iron and wood smoke.

Professor Munro even smells like he belongs out here in the ancient wilderness–with the addition of soap, I guess.

"It's a long flight home tomorrow."

I nod, trailing over to his bed. This room is slightly bigger than the others, with a woven rug spread over the floorboards and a large bay window hung with patterned curtains. Fancy.

"It doesn't feel like we're going home." I flop onto the bed, bouncing slightly on the hard mattress. "It feels like we're leaving it. To me, anyway."

"Ah, sweetheart." Cameron rounds the bed, then stares at me from above. His blue eyes look sad. "I never meant to upset you, Angie. I've been a very selfish man."

Well. That's that, then.

An answer to the question I wasn't quite brave enough to ask. I should never have wondered if we could keep this going—if we could have more.

"Sure." My throat is so tight, it comes out in a whisper. "I'm not upset." *Liar.* "And you're not selfish. I'm just glad we have another night together."

That part is true at least, and Professor Munro nods before kicking off his boots and climbing onto the bed next to me. Usually, we fall all over each other like starving animals, but tonight...

"Maybe I could just hold you for a while, Angie." He's already drawing me into his strong arms, already settling us back against the pillows and propping his chin on my head. His beard rasps against my hair. "The other stuff is wonderful too, but I'll be honest–this is what I'll miss the most."

I swallow hard, blinking back tears. "Yeah." My cheek pillows against his huge chest. "Me too, professor."

Because that's what he is. He's not *Cameron*, he's my history professor, and though I managed to forget that for a few days, I guess he never did.

We lie together for hours, sharing breaths and not speaking. And when I finally roll out of bed, hair mussed and heart breaking, he doesn't stop me. Professor Munro murmurs, "Goodnight, sweetheart," for the last time, and then...

He lets me go.

* * *

One dead-eyed flight.

Several long, exhausted hours in airports and vans and the college minibus, carrying us back to campus.

238

And one awkward exchange with Brian, when he lifts my lilac suitcase out of the back for me, then sweeps me into a rushed, bony hug under Professor Munro's watchful gaze.

"Take care of yourself, Angie."

I squeeze him back, bewildered. "Thanks, Brian."

He nods to the professor, then hitches his large backpack onto his shoulders and sets off into the maze of campus buildings. His overstuffed backpack sways as he walks, and we both watch him go, tired and bemused.

"Guess you made an impression." Professor Munro sounds dour, but not annoyed at anyone–except maybe himself. He rubs his bearded jaw, watching me with those blue eyes, and the early morning light brings out the shadows clinging beneath them.

"Jealous?" I want to ask him, plucking at the rolled sleeve of his shirt and tugging him closer until that frown melts away.

I don't. We're back to professor and student, and it's not my place.

For the first week back at college, I barely sleep. I'm a ghost of myself, drifting between lectures and the library, throwing myself into fevered study sessions to distract from the ache in my chest. I get more done in a week than I usually do in a month, but I can't slow down. Can't stop working. I can't afford to face reality just yet.

By the end of the second week, I'm sleeping again, on and off, but it's only slightly better. I always dream of *him*, and wake up with damp cheeks.

And after a month, I can see him in the hallways without wanting to weep. After two, I can kid myself that it wasn't a big deal–that I didn't lose something critically important when we left Scotland behind.

Sometimes I see Professor Munro on campus. I nod at him awkwardly in the coffee shop; I duck behind the library shelves to escape his view. It's weird every single time, my body brimming suddenly full of pain and relief and joy and longing.

Does he feel something, *anything*, when he sees me around?

Was it earth-shattering for him, too?

I can't tell.

So as graduation day approaches, I wait for it with determined numbness. After the last two months, it would be ridiculous to hope for anything from him. To think that once we're no longer professor and student, something might change.

What we had in Scotland was incredible.

But it's over now.

Angie

ow, despite all the fuss they get, graduation ceremonies are really freaking boring. It's just a series of dry speeches and a preachy commencement address, and then an endless list of graduates' names. We sit in rows on stage, draped in shapeless black robes, and wait for our time to be called while trying not to yawn in front of the big crowd.

And when we *are* called, it's all over in a handful of seconds. We stumble across the stage, trying not to trip. We take our diploma from one professor, and shake hands with another.

That last part is the bit that gets me most, because it's not just *any* professor. I am very well acquainted with this man's hands.

"Congratulations, Angie." Professor Munro squeezes my fingers gently. His grip is big and warm and perfect and *god.* My stomach swoops like I'm on a roller coaster. "You've done so well."

I nod and force my legs to work again, carrying me to the

other side of the stage. I'm wobbly as a baby deer, and it's a relief to make it back to safety.

My hand tingles where he touched me as I slide back into my seat. I fiddle with my diploma.

It didn't mean anything. Professor Munro is shaking everyone's hands.

Get it together, Angie Kim.

Most graduates wander off with their parents after the ceremony, going to take photos and eat expensive dinners. My parents offered to come today, but missing work would have made things difficult for them, so I told them we'd celebrate together soon instead.

I'm kind of regretting that decision now. As I trail past families and couples in my stupid robes, I've never felt so freaking lonely.

Maybe that's why I go there: to the history department. It's not like he'll *be* there, but I'd like to see his office one more time before I leave for good. For old times' sake.

I wander past glass cases of pottery and coins. Past a stuffed fox, posed morbidly on a flat stone. And for once, the history department is *silent*.

No hum of a distant lecture. No rattling radiators. No thundering footsteps of a crowd.

Nothing.

The other notable lack? There's no line outside Professor Munro's office. He may be a big deal on campus, may have admirers everywhere, but for once, I trudge straight to the door.

I prod it with a finger. I don't expect it to swing open, and I gape at the man hunched behind his desk, face buried in his hands.

"Professor Munro?"

His face stays in his hands, but his fingers part. Blue eyes peer through them at me, and he frowns like he thinks I'm not real.

"Angie? What are you doing here, sweetheart?"

He's taken his fancy professor robes off, tossing them on top of a filing cabinet. Instead, he's back to his usual fare: a worn, soft-looking red flannel shirt and jeans.

"Um." I risk a few steps inside the office. The door clicks shut quietly behind me. "Reminiscing, I guess."

Professor Munro grunts, and he finally takes his hands away, leaning back in his chair. He looks more rumpled, more exhausted than usual. Is he sleeping okay?

"I always liked your visits," he admits. "Sometimes I thought I was going mad, dreaming you up in here. Like a pretty little vision, come to brighten up my days."

I snort. "Sounds like carbon monoxide poisoning."

Professor Munro blinks, and then he tips his head back and booms out his signature laughter. And it's so good to make him laugh, to see him and hear his voice and be this close, and I can't help it. I stumble forward a few steps.

The laughter fades, but he's still grinning. "Ah, Angie. I hoped I might see you one last time. I know I don't deserve it, but I hoped for it all the same."

One last time?

Does it have to be that?

I bite my lip, hovering in the center of his office. And maybe Scotland made me braver, or maybe it's that I'm a graduate now, or maybe it's just that I have nothing left to lose. But I hear my own voice fill the room, clear as day.

"I wanted to see you too, but not for one last time, professor.

I *always* want to see you."

Professor Munro's face crumples. "Sweetheart. Fuck. I missed you."

He pushes to his feet as I stumble round his desk. We collide like comets, like continents, like forces of nature that can't be held back, and the professor holds me so tightly, he might never let go.

It's a hug at first. Then his head turns, cautious and seeking, and I answer him with a hard kiss.

I've missed him.

God, I've missed him so much.

I've been wandering around with my heart left behind in this office.

"Angie." He breaks away, chest heaving, and spins me around until my ass nudges the desk. Two big hands grip my waist, and then I'm boosted up, heels swinging in the empty air. "Fuck. Angie. My Angie."

"Professor–"

"Cameron," he growls, tugging at the fastenings on my graduation robes. "Shit, I hate these stupid robes. Doesn't matter. Call me Cameron, sweetheart, please."

"Cameron." I draw myself up. Determined. "I want more this time."

Cautious eyes flick up to mine, then back down to his work. The first fastening slips free. The second. "More of my body?"

Damn. "Yes, definitely that. But more of the rest of it, too."

Those big hands slow against my robes. And his jaw works like he's trying out questions. Chewing over what to say. "Whatever you want, you can have it, Angie. But can you tell a muddled old man what you mean?"

"You're not old," I say automatically. Then: "Um. I don't

know. I guess I'd like to go on a date? If that's okay?"

"If that's…" Cameron trails off, huffing a laugh. "Of course it's okay. But why would a beautiful girl like you want to date a man like me?"

I stiffen, affronted on his behalf. "What is *that* supposed to mean?"

Cameron says nothing, suddenly hyper-focused on my robes, and they come undone easily, sagging down my shoulders. I pull my arms out, the black fabric pooling around me on the desk, but I don't stop staring at him. I won't let him out of this.

"Cameron."

"Hm?"

"Look, if you don't want to date me, that's fine. But–"

"Of course I want to," he snaps, and it's his turn to sound annoyed. "I'm a professor, Angie, not a fucking moron. I know a–a *goddess* when I've found one. If I had my way, I wouldn't just date you, either; I'd snatch you up and carry you to the nearest chapel. I'd marry you on the spot, sweetheart, and keep you forever. But you deserve better, don't you see that? And–*Angie*. Why are you laughing, damn it?"

"I don't know," I wheeze. "I'm happy, I guess."

He wants to marry me?

Holy crap. Well, the feeling's mutual. And maybe the future is uncertain, maybe there are big questions looming like jobs and careers and where to live, but one thing is rock-solid in my mind.

I want this man.

He wants me.

And I've graduated. There's nothing standing in our way anymore.

"Here. Come here." I tug at his belt, pulling him to stand between my thighs. I wore a blue silk sheath dress for graduation, and it hitches up, baring my legs as I shuffle them wider. "Let's do all that stuff. I'm in. I'm so in. But first-"

"Yeah." Cameron grips my thighs, his gaze roving hungrily down my body. "*First.* You're right."

The office door's not locked, but who's going to come in? And even if they did, would we stop? Would we care? I don't think so, not right now.

Not with Cameron's big, warm hands scorching paths over my skin until my nipples jut against my dress. Not when he ducks his head, sucking on them through the silk as I groan and tug at his belt.

I've never touched him like this. He never let me, and I half expect him to stop me now. But he doesn't, he even twists his hips to give me a better angle, and then I'm drawing his cock out into the air.

It's thick. Flushed at the tip, with a vein running up one side. A bead of moisture leaks from the head, and I spread it carefully with my thumb.

A hiss. Cameron stiffens. "*Fuck.* Angie, go easy on me, sweetheart. Don't make a fool out of me now." I'm not sure what he's babbling about, and I don't care. All I know is, back in Scotland, he licked between my thighs until I could barely see straight, and now it's my turn.

The desk creaks as I lean forward. Cameron curses under his breath, but he gathers my long hair back and holds it for me at my nape.

I run my tongue up the base of his cock. He tastes salty. And clean. And *good.*

I might not have done this before, but I know the general

idea. I grip the base of his shaft in one hand, grabbing his hip for balance with the other, and I draw the head into my mouth, suckling on it for all I'm worth.

"Angie! Fucking hell."

I bob my head. I swirl my tongue. I peer up at the professor through hazy eyes. I'd do this for hours if he let me, but when he snaps, cursing loudly and nudging me to sit up, I lift my hips eagerly as he tugs my panties down my legs.

"This might hurt the first time." Cameron crowds close, flipping my dress further up my thighs. His cock bobs between us, flushed and ready and wet with my saliva. "I'll be gentle. Fuck. Angie, are you sure? We can wait. We can do this differently."

He breaks off with a groan as I grip his cock, gently tugging him closer. "I'm sure."

He still kisses me first, deep and slow. Like we have all the time in the world. Like he really would tuck himself away without a single ounce of bitterness if I told him to.

Cameron Munro is such a good man. The knowledge coasts through me, warm and golden, as I guide him between my thighs.

The first press is intense. My breath freezes in my lungs; my legs stiffen where they're wrapped around his waist. But Cameron rubs his palm over my back, murmuring soothing words, and he waits until I've melted against him before he nudges forward again, his thick cock pushing deeper inside.

Push. Freeze. Soothing words. Repeat. On and on, his cock wedging deeper and deeper inside me. And if my inexperience is annoying for him, he doesn't show it. Cameron kisses me hard, *desperately*, his hands roaming over every inch of me that he can touch.

With every touch, every kiss, every nip of his teeth, I get slicker between my legs. More flushed, more hungry for him, until I'm rocking my hips up, impatient, urging him on, and with a broken laugh, Cameron thrusts all the way inside me.

God.

I'm so *full*.

Impaled on his cock, and I can feel it throbbing inside me. Can feel his *pulse*.

"Okay, sweetheart?"

I nod, teeth chattering. "Yeah. Yes. I just—I need you to *move*."

Cameron

I need you to move.

God. I couldn't deny this girl anything, but that? It's already a done deal. From the moment I slid inside her tight, wet heat, there was no other way this could go.

"Hold on to me."

Angie wraps her arms around my neck. I roll my hips–slowly at first, then gathering speed. Thrusting faster, harder, *deeper*. She's gripping me so tight, legs cinched around my waist, and her grunts and breathy little moans are music to my ears.

She's so fucking beautiful, her silk dress rippling over her curves like water, and I smell fresh cotton and lemons, and *god*. This is happening.

"Angie. Sweetheart." I don't know what I'm saying. Don't know anything except the hot slide of my cock and the sinful wet noises between us. "Angel. You feel so good."

"S-so do you."

I grit my teeth, forcing my head back to stare at her. Making sure she means it, but yeah—she's glassy-eyed, her pupils blown wide. Angie's flushed and rumpled, clinging to me like a life raft in a storm, and the desk creaks madly as she lifts her hips, slamming herself harder and harder on my shaft.

"You like that?"

"Uh-huh." If she keeps biting her lip like that, she'll draw blood. I duck my head, kissing her instead, thrusting my tongue against hers. And I swallow every moan she gives me, greedy for them.

Fuck.

I slow down for a second, breath ragged, and shift my hips, screwing my cock into every fluttering inch of her channel. I want to savor her, damn it. I want to feel her skin heating under my palms; want to wedge myself so deep inside her that she'll never stop feeling me there. And Angie's everything I dreamed of when I jerked my cock to thoughts of her for the last few years—she's so wet, so needy, so fucking delicious.

"Faster." Her fingernails dig into my shoulders. She tugs on me, legs squeezing around my hips. "Take me faster again. Make me feel it tomorrow."

Jesus Christ. My Angie is wild, and I love it. I up the pace, muscles burning and heart slamming, and fuck her so hard that my desk shudders over the office floor.

Come on.

Come for me.

There's barely any room between our bodies, but I cram a hand between us, reaching between her legs. Everything's a muddle of slick thighs and plunging cock and the pale blue silk of her dress, but I find her clit and rub quick circles. Angie's eyes flutter closed, and I keep thrusting, keep rubbing, my whole body an exposed nerve under my clothes.

"Cameron."

She clamps down on me like a vice. Tremors shudder through her, and I feel them from the inside out, massaging me, *milking* me.

With a groan, I surrender. Spill floods of wet heat deep inside.

We come back to the earth slowly, spinning down like autumn leaves. A stray hair sticks to the corner of Angie's mouth again, and with a breathless laugh, I brush it away. I'm still inside her, softening now, but I can't bring myself to step back.

"You still in, Angie Kim?" With the rest of it, I mean. The dates and the chapel and my carrying her over my shoulder into the sunset. I know she agreed, but I won't hold her to it. Not if she's changed her mind.

But she rolls her eyes and pins me with a smile. She grips two handfuls of my shirt, squeezing damp creases into the fabric.

"Are you trying to get rid of me again, Professor Munro?"

"Never." It sounds like a vow. It *is* a vow. "If you want me, you've got me."

Her forehead drops against my shoulder. I rub circles on her back, marveling at the pounding of her heart. "It's settled, then," Angie says, her voice muffled, and I bury my smile in her hair.

It's settled. Yeah. That works for me.

I don't know how I got so lucky, but I'll happily pledge my life to Angie Kim.

* * *

Thanks for reading the Big Boys! I hope you loved these burly dreamboats. :)

For another instalove box set check out Winter Warmers: Books 1-6. I promise: they're hot enough to melt the snowbank.

And for a bonus instalove story, grab your copy of Beauty & The Kingpin. *I'm a florist. He's the king of the underworld.*

Happy reading!

xxx

Teaser: Winter Ward

The last time I stepped foot in this house, I must have been ten years old. I remember staring open-mouthed at the high ceilings and glittering chandeliers; remember rocking up onto my toes to try to see the oil paintings lining the walls. As a child, Herr Vogel's townhouse seemed more like a museum than a home—all cold marble and heavy drape curtains, a quiet hush permeating through the halls.

At twenty, I like to think I am harder to intimidate. Less likely to lose my tongue when Herr Vogel speaks to me.

But I still packed a few extra sweaters in my suitcase, ready for the cold composer and his even colder townhouse.

"My housekeeper prepared a guest suite for you."

I follow a set of broad shoulders up the winding staircase, noting the way Herr Vogel's tailored white shirt clings to his body. Is it so very physical, composing music? Where the hell did all those muscles come from? The man is lean with a narrow waist, but even through his shirt, he seems harder than marble. Like he could hop up onto a plinth in one of the alcoves and blend in with the other sculptures.

"That was kind of her."

A pair of light gray eyes glance back at me. "Indeed."

I'm glad Herr Vogel is leading the way rather than walking beside me. It lets me stare at him openly, comparing this man to the figure in my memory. He is as tall as I remembered, towering above me, but his black hair is longer, brushing at his collar, and dusted with silver at the temples. His voice, in the rare instance that he speaks, is low and husky, and his hand is strong where it grips my suitcase handle.

Our fingers brushed when he took it from me. I never noticed hands as a little girl, but as a twenty year old woman…

Herr Vogel has beautiful hands.

"I work long hours." Herr Vogel does not turn his head as he speaks, instead addressing the empty hallway in front of us. Doors slip past on either side, and still we keep walking, steps sinking into the dark green rug. "My work must not be disturbed. Do you understand?"

God, why do these men keep asking me that? Do they truly think it is so complicated? Maybe *I* don't want to be disturbed either.

I purse my lips. "I understand."

"However long you plan to stay here—"

"Three weeks, I believe."

He shrugs one shoulder, as if it doesn't matter. "However long you stay, you have access to the full house. All except for my private quarters, of course, and the music room."

My heart sinks. I clutch my violin case closer. *The music room.*

"Of course."

What did I expect? That I'd play endless duets with a famous composer? That he would take an interest in me, *teach* me, even allow me to listen to him working?

Ridiculous. I'm here as a favor to my father, nothing more. Herr Vogel understands that, even if I tried to forget it. Even if for a foolish moment, I let some excitement slip through.

This is not some musician's vacation.

I'm here because I have nowhere else to go.

* * *

Check out Winter Ward and the other Winter Warmers!

xxx

Cassie Mint

About the Author

Cassie writes outrageous, OTT instalove with tons of sugar and spice. She loves cookie dough, summer barbecues, and her gorgeous cat Missy.

You can connect with me on:
🌐 https://www.authorcassiemint.com
📘 https://www.facebook.com/cassiemintauthor
🔗 https://www.bookbub.com/authors/cassie-mint

Subscribe to my newsletter:
✉ https://www.authorcassiemint.com/newsletter

www.ingramcontent.com/pod-product-compliance
Lightning Source LLC
Chambersburg PA
CBHW011432170626
46808CB00010B/3126

* 9 7 8 1 9 1 5 7 3 5 1 6 4 *